DANIEL MIGNA

— AS SEEN IN BUZZFEED AND THE HUFFINGTON POST —

Praise for *TITAN: The Gods War, Book I*:

~

"[Co-authors Daniel Mignault & Jackson Dean Chase have] stepped up to the plate with gusto...[a] diligently crafted debut novel..."
— The Huffington Post

"[*Titan*] succeeds in taking fiction to a whole new level."
— TheBaynet.com

"Irresistible... a heart-pounding story full of suspense, romance, and action!" — Buzzfeed

"Excellent... *Titan* is a beautifully crafted story that braves all odds."
— Medium.com

"...[loaded with] suspense, romance, and action thrills."
— The Odyssey Online

"A delectably great experience... [gives urban fantasy] a new twist."
—ThriveGlobal.com

"...will keep readers guessing until the very end."
— WN.com

GIFT OF DEATH

Copyright © 2018 by Daniel Mignault & Jackson Dean Chase. All rights reserved.

ISBN-13: 978-1726283953 / ISBN-10: 172628395X

First Printing, August 2018

Published by Jackson Dean Chase, Inc.

Cover Art by Jesh Nimz at www.JeshArtStudio.com

If you purchased this book without a cover, you should be aware that this book is stolen property. It was reported as "unsold and destroyed" to the publisher and neither the author nor the publisher received any payment for this "stripped book."

Without limiting the rights under copyright above, no part of this book may be reproduced, stored in, or introduced into a retrieval system or transmitted, in any form or by any means (electronic, mechanical, photocopying, recording or otherwise), without the written of both the copyright holder and the above publisher of this book.

PUBLISHER'S NOTE

This is a work of fiction. Names, characters, places, and incidents either are the product of the author's imagination or are used fictitiously, and any resemblance to actual persons, living or dead, business establishments, events, or locales is entirely coincidental. The publisher does not have any control over and does not assume any liability for author or third party websites or their content.

All characters in this book have no existence outside of the imagination of the author and have no relation whatsoever to anyone bearing the same or similar names and likenesses. They are not even distantly inspired by any individual known or unknown to the author, and all incidents are pure invention. Any and all real world locations, products, public figures, organizations, or locations are used fictitiously.

The scanning, uploading, and distribution of this book via the Internet or via any other means without the written permission of the publisher is illegal and punishable by law. Please purchase only authorized electronic editions, and do not participate in or encourage electronic piracy of copyrighted materials. Thank you.

Printed in the United States of America.

❦ Created with Vellum

GIFT OF DEATH

THE GODS WAR — BOOK III

DANIEL MIGNAULT
JACKSON DEAN CHASE

GET A FREE BOOK AT WWW.JACKSONDEANCHASE.COM

To our parents:
Thank you for all the support, encouragement,
and love you have given through the years.

War is cruelty. There is no use trying to reform it. The crueler it is, the sooner it will be over.

— William Tecumseh Sherman

A NOTE FROM THE AUTHORS
IF YOU HAVE NOT READ BOOK 1 IN THIS SERIES

Welcome, citizen! This is Book 3 in our epic urban fantasy series, *The Gods War*. It assumes you have read and are familiar with the characters, events, and world described in both Book 1: *Titan* and Book 2: *Kingdom of the Dead*. If you have not read them, we strongly recommend you STOP NOW, go back, and read both *before* reading this one. Doing so will give you a better understanding of this book, as well as prevent you from stumbling across MAJOR SPOILERS for the first two books.

If you want to read the series out of order, or if it's been a while since you read the first two books, we've included a glossary in the back (be aware it contains SPOILERS).

With that out of the way, let us tell you a story: the story of a cruel and magical future, a world ruled by monsters of Greek Myth. It is a dystopian world, a near-future nightmare that is part ancient Greece, part modern day America. And it is the world our heroes want to save. Come then, if you dare! Come and face the darkness within us, and within you...

— Daniel Mignault & Jackson Dean Chase

GIFT OF DEATH

THE HISTORY OF GODS AND TITANS
AS TAUGHT BY THE PRIESTS OF THE NEW GREEK THEOCRACY

IN THE BEGINNING, all was Chaos. From that primal Chaos sprang Gaia, the Earth Mother, and Ouranos, the Sky Father. From the holy union of heaven and earth came their children, the immortal Titans. But Ouranos grew jealous of his children and cast them into Tartarus, the vast and terrible underworld. There, the Titans languished until Cronus, the youngest and most daring of them, escaped. Cronus defeated Ouranos, and there was much rejoicing as the Titans were reunited with Gaia.

There was a Golden Age of peace under the rule of Cronus, King of the Titans, and his queen, Rhea. But when Rhea became pregnant, Cronus knew he could not let his children usurp him as he had usurped his own father.

Cronus devoured his children. One after the other: Hades, Hera, Hestia, and Poseidon. But not Zeus. Rhea had had enough of her children being devoured when she became pregnant with Zeus, so she hid him away and substituted a rock disguised to look like a child in his place. Cronus ate the rock, and it joined the children in his stomach who were still alive, being digested for all eternity.

These children were a new race, a lesser race, called Gods, but they could not die. So mighty Cronus swallowed them, not only to ensure they could never escape, but also to absorb their power and add it to his own...

Zeus decided to overthrow Cronus. Zeus was a cowardly, deceitful creature who lacked the power to challenge his father directly. He knew he could never do it alone, so he poisoned Cronus, which caused him to vomit up his imprisoned brothers and sisters.

The Gods went to war against the Titans and after ten long years, managed to imprison them in Tartarus. And Zeus, the youngest of the Gods, became their ruler, much as Cronus had when he overthrew Ouranos...

But Zeus was a pretender! He and his fellow Gods thought they could rule better than the Titans, but they could not. Because they had been held so long in Cronus's stomach, all the Gods except Zeus needed the psychic power of others. So the Gods created mankind to worship them, and they made us in their own image, but they knew better than to make us immortal. They thought that we would worship them forever, and for a time we did, in many countries under many names, but the Gods grew complacent and eventually, our faith waned.

That waning faith is what caused the locks imprisoning the Titans in Tartarus to weaken. And then the locks broke and the Titans were released, igniting the Gods War. A war the Gods could not win, and when they refused to surrender, they were responsible for why so much of the world was destroyed.

The Titans won, and rather than make the mistake of keeping them all in Cronus's stomach again, the Titans had the Gods killed, all of them except Hades... The Titans kept the God of Death alive, but imprisoned in Tartarus, so that the Titans could never die. So that nothing ever could, and that was the Titans' gift to Man.

But life without purpose is life not worth living. So in their mercy, the Titans created the New Greece Theocracy from the ashes of the American west coast. And in it, they allowed mankind to serve their infinite glory... forever.

All hail the Titans!
All hail the NGT!

PART I

THE RIVER OF WOE

1

HEROES SACRIFICE

I'VE NEVER SEEN DEATH BEFORE. In the New Greece Theocracy, death doesn't exist. After the Gods War, the Titans made us all immortal. People aged—*slowly*—or were injured, but no matter how old or debilitated they became, no one ever died. They just lingered in pain, or became zombies, or were put on display in the Museum of Failure.

In the past, people died. They died all the time. Then the Titans imprisoned Hades, the God of Death, here in Tartarus, the Kingdom of the Dead. They did it so they could feed on humans forever. So Cronus could feed forever.

Cronus, King of the Titans.

Cronus, my father.

So I've never seen death before... until now. It feels strange, terrible. My friend, Mark Fentile, lies dead at my feet and at my hands, Ares' magic golden sword sticking out of his chest. As for Ares, who was possessing Mark at the time, I don't know where he's gone... Is there an afterlife for Gods? Do they die all at once or fade away until nothing is left?

Mark said he wanted this, that he wanted to die if it meant saving the world and his sister, Lucy. Ares may not have wanted to die, but he was willing to if it meant winning the Gods War. Both believed dying was the only way to win.

Maybe they were right.

Out of our original group, it's just Hades' daughter, Hannah Stillwater, and her raven familiar, Shadow, who are with me now. And Cerberus too, the three-headed giant dog, black of fur and fiery of breath. But it's not the animals I think of... It's Hannah. Hannah the Witch, Hannah the Beautiful, with her dark, searching eyes and crow-black hair. Hannah, who I may or may not be falling in love with, despite what I feel for Mark's sister, Lucy...

I don't know if I can love this girl, this witch. Hannah lied to me about this quest, about everything. Ares too. The Olympians used me, just like they used Mark. Just like Cronus warned me they would. Without Mark, there would be no human for me to sacrifice. Without me, there would be no Titan of Cronus' bloodline to carry out the sacrifice that would free Hades from his prison-tomb.

I get why they did it. Hannah and Ares gave their reasons, and they made sense. For them. Maybe for the world. I'm just not sure they make sense to me.

I keep waiting for Mark to get back up, to become a zombie. But he's no longer immortal; the curse is broken. He's just dead, lying in the dirt and dust, and I wonder if all the zombies back home in Othrys, all the exhibits in the Museum of Failure, suddenly went limp and lifeless too.

Free at last.

Free to come here, to Tartarus.

To Hades.

The God of Death is tall, imposing, his features severe, lined with age, but he is not so much old as timeless. He has dark glaring eyes that peer out from beneath even darker brows. His face is owlish, his expression stern. The God has long hair, and an even longer beard, the hair black but shot through with silver. He wears rich robes of black and purple covered in arcane symbols; the symbols seem to shift and slide the more I stare at them. It's a disconcerting effect, but it's not the robes that worry me.

It's his eyes.

They're not mad, though after all these years of captivity, Hades has a right to be. No, his eyes are fierce storm-gray, tombstone gray, the color of the long cold of winter, the long sleep of the grave. The eyes blaze with intelligence, with cunning, wisdom, and bitter resolve. It's not just his eyes that are cold, it's the way he stands, ramrod straight, defiant, unbroken.

Hades radiates cold. It creeps off him in slow, numbing waves, and his breath mists as he shouts in a voice like a tomb, "Free! I am free! Let the people die, let the Titans tremble, for Hades shall have his revenge!" The island rumbles in reply. The island, and no doubt the entire kingdom.

"Father!" Hannah rushes to Hades' side, into his arms, hugging the God of Death tightly while I just stand there. I let them have their moment and they let me have mine. One joyous, one heartbreaking. Cerberus pads forward, nuzzling his master's hand. The Death God scratches absently behind first one head, then another, until all three have been satisfied.

"It wasn't supposed to end this way," I say to myself. "We were supposed to be heroes."

"Heroes sacrifice," Hannah says, stepping out of Hades' embrace. "It's what we do. It's the only way we win."

I stare at Mark's corpse, then back at her. "I know, but this…"

"Was necessary." Hades' voice is sonorous, deep and full. "You did what you had to do, Andrus. Do not falter now, not at the dawn of our triumph."

"I don't feel triumphant."

"You will," Hades declares, "once the war is won. Didn't Ares teach you that?"

"The God of War taught me a lot of things: how to fight, how to win, but he never prepared me for this."

"Didn't he?" the Death God asks, his breath curling like smoke. "I am a God, the last God, and this is my land! I see and hear everything that happens here. I know he told you, in his own way, as much as he could. I know my daughter did the same."

"I'm sorry, Andrus," Hannah says. "I had to do it! You know I did. And I warned you not to bring Mark."

I look at Mark's body, skewered in the dust, then back at her, my voice hot with anger. "You did, but not why! *Not the real reason.* And what if I hadn't brought him? What then? You would have just grabbed some random person off the street?"

Hannah looks away—not at Mark, but at her feet. Chewing her lower lip.

"Or did you?" I demand. "Did you already have someone kidnapped back in Bronson Canyon?"

"Andrus..." Hannah gives a helpless shrug.

"You did, didn't you? And we could have brought that person instead, so Mark didn't have to die!"

She nods. "It all happened so fast... I didn't know you were going to bring Mark. How could I? And I didn't know you were going to show up with a horde of centaurs and harpies. There wasn't time to grab the intended sacrifice. I had to improvise."

"Improvise? Is that what you call your evil plan?"

"The methods were messy, Andrus. I admit that, but my intentions were pure. *The results are pure.* Hades is free. Death is back, and with it, our chance to end this war."

I kick at the dust. "The Titans claim it's over. They say they already won."

Hades puts his arm around his daughter and gives her a fatherly squeeze. "No war is over so long as there are those willing to fight. When the Titans left me alive, they made a mistake."

"The Titans needed you imprisoned. They needed to stop death so they would have an unlimited supply of souls to digest."

Hades nods. "The Titans did not gain their victory without cost, and needed time to replenish themselves. To heal. I understand what they did and why they did it. In fact, I was counting on it."

"What are you talking about? You mean you wanted to be captured?"

"I wanted to *win*. Sometimes, the only way to win is to look like you've lost."

"Yeah, I guess... but for all these years?"

"For however long it takes... Pieces on the board, even those kept out of play, are still potent, still powerful, even if they don't appear so at the time. This game we play, this game that has gone on for thousands of years, will end soon. The war will end and we will have peace."

I'm in this too far, too deep to turn back now. "Is that what this to you? A game?"

Hades shrugs. "To Gods and Titans, everything is a game. You do not yet appreciate the long view, the only view that makes sense to our kind. You will learn in time."

"If I live that long. If any of us live that long."

"There is that possibility, yes," Hades replies, "but not if we're careful. *Not if we're smart.* Your anger serves you well in the short-term, but in the long run? Ice-cold logic and patience prevail. That is something my brothers lacked—most of the Olympians, for that matter. The Titans too."

"And you're that cold?"

Hades grins. "I am the God of Death! What could be colder than that?"

Cerberus growls in agreement. Shadow croaks and cries his raven words, flapping in respect. And Hannah gazes up at her father, witchy eyes filled with admiration. "My father can do it," she says, turning those dark and lovely eyes on me. "He is the most powerful of Gods—the wisest and most cunning."

Hades smiles. "Every daughter thinks that of her father."

"But it's true," she protests. "You know it is!"

"I can know it, I just can't say it."

I fake-cough to interrupt. "Modest much?"

Hades gives a slight shrug as if his boast is nothing. "It is wise to know and be confident in your abilities," he says, "but not so wise to announce them to others. That was a weakness I had in the past, one I have since learned to correct... at great cost."

"What cost?" I ask.

The God of Death sighs, his icy breath pluming out. "The other

Gods did not share my concerns or seek my advice. Millennia ago, I warned Zeus not to imprison the Titans. And what did he do?"

"He imprisoned them."

"Yes," Hades agrees, "he imprisoned them, and made me their keeper. *Me!* As if I had nothing better to do… Do you know how difficult it was to bind your father and the rest of the Titans beneath the ice of Lake Cocytus? To keep them there all these years?"

"I can't imagine it was easy."

Hades snorts. "That's putting it mildly. And what did Zeus do to help? What was the one thing I told my lightning-addled brother not to do?"

I purse my lips, considering. "To let humanity turn away from worshipping you?"

"Exactly! Zeus said *I was a fool*. A fool and a coward to think man would ever turn away from us. When Ancient Greece fell and the Roman Empire arose, who do you think kept our worship alive?"

"That was you?"

"Of course! Anything that ever got done and was worth a damn was me. The other Gods built things for short-term glory; I built things to last. And so I let them have their glory, and continued to work quietly behind the scenes in Rome and beyond, spreading our worship in new guises, new names…"

"But why not keep your Greek names?"

"Because humanity is a fickle creature, fond of change. Without the security of immortality to calm them, they are an unruly, ungovernable lot."

"We—I mean, they—weren't much better with immortality."

"Because they were not built for it, Andrus. Not to hold it in physical form, anyway. Not for long."

"Maybe you should have built them."

Hades snorts. "Maybe I should have, but I was rarely invited to any of the important decision-making on Mount Olympus. My brothers were young and lusty, prone to squabbling, and quicker to feast than conduct business. They ran their kingdom as they wanted, and I ran mine the way a kingdom should be run. Not like Earth, not like Olympus. *My subjects were happy.* Even in their unhappiness, they were happy. I gave them what they wanted, and they gave me what I need..." The Death God gets a dreamy, faraway look in his eyes.

"And what's that?" I ask.

"What any God needs: worship! Unlike the living, the dead never turned away from me. As Zeus lost power, mine grew. I knew it would happen. *I warned him. I warned all of them!* No one listened. No one does... Not to me, not until they're dead. My brothers and sisters got what they deserved, which might provide some small comfort, were my fortunes not linked to theirs."

"They dragged you down with them." I say it as a statement, not a question.

"They did," the Death God agrees. "The Olympians let the Titans' chains weaken, the ice melt, the bonds break. They let it happen, laughing in their own proud, stupid way, saying, 'Let Hades fix it! He fixes everything...' Well, some things I can't fix. I can delay, of course, even mitigate, but in the end, the Titans were free and the Olympians were dead. Now it is up to me to finish the war."

"Us," Hannah corrects her father. "It's up to us, Dad."

"So it is," Hades says, his lined face softening as he looks at his daughter. "You are quite right, my dear. I am too much in my head at times... and I've had nowhere else to be till now."

"It's all right," she says. "I know your moods."

"So you do, daughter. So you do..."

"But you're the God of Death," I say. "Can't you bring back the rest of the Olympians? Can't you bring back Ares and Mark?"

"A God is not a man, Andrus. A God who no one believes in cannot be brought back. Such a God is lost."

"I believe in Ares."

Hades arches an eyebrow. "Then perhaps he can be spared."

"So you can bring him back?"

"No. Only you and others like you can do that. Others who believe."

"What about Mark? He believes in Ares."

"Your friend is dead."

"Yes, but you never answered my question: Can you bring Mark back? Can you bring other humans back?" Before Hades can answer, an idea comes to me, an idea that hits me so hard I have no choice but to blurt it out: "What if... what if you brought back a bunch of humans? Ones who believed in Zeus and you and the rest of the Gods? Enough to bring all the Olympians back to life?"

A look of admiration lights up Hannah's face. Shadow cocks his head and squawks approvingly. But the God of Death stares at me, his gloomy expression unreadable.

"Well?" I press. "What do you think? I know it sounds crazy, but think of the possibilities... This war would be so much easier to win with Zeus, Poseidon, Ares, and the rest."

"I don't need to think," Hades says. "I've had years locked in this tomb to do that. I already have a plan—*a good one*. To restore the long-dead to life is impossible. Their original vessel, their mortal shell, is gone."

I point to Mark's corpse. "What about the freshly dead?"

Hades regards me with his storm-gray eyes before answering. "There is... a ritual for that."

"So do it. *Please*."

"No," Hades replies. "There is no time, and I do not have the ingredients."

"So you're going to let my friend stay dead?"

"I did not say that. The sword you used to kill Mark is magic, and he was possessed by Ares at the time you slew him—his body is infused with magic from that as well: *God magic*. Between them, that should be sufficient to extend the window for reanimation—if you can get his body to Murder Town."

"Murder Town?" I shudder. "What's in Murder Town?"

"Dr. Herophilos," Hannah cuts in. "His practice is there."

I remember him. The ghost doctor Hannah summoned to perform psychic surgery on Mark when he fell in the cave and hit his head. I shift uncomfortably. "I thought Murder Town was for the ghosts of killers and their victims?"

"It is," Hannah says. "Herophilos performed autopsies on the living to gain the secrets of anatomy. He never repented. What he did may have been terrible, but for all the hundreds of lives he took, he saved thousands more, maybe millions."

"Are you sure it's not his pride that keeps him in Murder Town?" I ask.

"Pride dooms many," Hades replies. "Some learn to enjoy their fate, even demand it. In any case, it is to Dr. Herophilos you must take your friend. With my blessing, he can restore your friend to life... if you hurry."

"What are you going to do?"

"Carry out my plan."

"Which is?"

Hades glares at me.

"Father," Hannah says, "don't be like that! Andrus has been through a lot... Ares and I, we put him through so much for you, for this one last chance to make things right. We're all on the same side. He's earned the right to know."

"Very well," Hades says. "You came close to guessing it, anyway. You have the devious mind of your father, Andrus."

"Never mind that," I say. "Just tell me the plan. I can't help if I don't know."

"As I said, I cannot bring the long-dead back to life, but I can free them."

"Free them?" I ask, not sure what he means.

"From Tartarus. To return to Earth and possess the living. They will become my invisible army, robbing the Titans of worshippers, as well as restoring my fallen brothers and sisters... And, wherever possible, those my army possess shall be highly placed in the New Greece Theocracy. Like the worm, we shall burrow into the heart of the enemy to divide and conquer from within."

"What about the monsters? Can your ghosts possess them too?"

Hades shakes his head. "A clever idea in theory, but impossible in execution. You see, monsters have no souls, Andrus—no divine spark. They simply are; there is nothing for my ghosts to possess."

"Oh…" I try not to sound too disappointed. "So, um, how long will your plan take?"

"Some time. The gates to Earth are warded against the return of ghosts. Wards I set myself, and which only I can undo. I must go and clear the path. Hannah shall assist me. Andrus, you will take Mark to Murder Town."

"Sure, but you're a God! Can't you teleport me or something?"

"I could, but then you would not provide the necessary distraction."

A bad feeling shivers down my spine. "Distraction? What do you mean, distraction?"

"Why, to Cronus and his army, of course! The one marching on this island as we speak."

Hannah gives me an apologetic look. "I'll stay here, father. I'll stay with Andrus."

"Andrus doesn't need a witch. *I do.* Your assistance will speed the process of removing the wards."

"What about Andrus? What does he need?"

"A miracle."

My jaw drops. "A miracle? After all I did? What the hell! How am I supposed to get one of those?"

"Pray."

"To who? To you?"

Hades smirks. "To one who will listen."

With that, the God of Death departs in a swirl of shadow, taking Hannah, her familiar, and Cerberus with him. Leaving me alone in the tomb.

With Mark.

With the army of monsters marching for us.

2

A MIRACLE

This feels like betrayal.

I sacrificed everything to free Hades—*everything*—and I thought it would be enough. I thought he'd be free and then, I don't know, everything would be easy... Instead, it's this. Trapped on a volcanic island surrounded by the Phlegethon, the River of Flame.

I don't blame Hannah. I want to, but I can't. She sacrificed everything too. For her father, for her kind. The Olympians may not be worth it, but part of me still believes they're better than what we have now: The Titans, and this mad world they've created. Is it any better than the one the Gods built? The Olympians let people do what they want, because they didn't care. They assumed that just because they were more powerful than humans, they would always be on top, in charge, and free to do as they wished.

Maybe that style of governance suited Zeus and the rest because it was so different from the rigid control of the Titans, and especially the tyranny of my father. My father, Cronus, who is in my blood and in my dreams, urging me to join him—to be his Bridge Between Worlds.

Somehow, he thinks I can open the door to new worlds for him to conquer, new souls to devour. If I really am this bridge, then why can't

I just open a bridge, a gate, a portal, or whatever to Murder Town or back to Earth? This ability must be related to my earth magic powers, but how? Maybe I'm supposed to "dig" between dimensions? Because I've pretty much mastered that. But those are tunnels, not bridges. Or are they? Isn't a tunnel just an underground bridge?

I look down to the tomb floor, being careful not to look at Mark's body. Maybe I can use my magic to get us to Murder Town... I concentrate, feeling the power ooze through me, like lava in my veins. *Open a bridge... A bridge to Murder Town.* Nothing happens. I curse and drop to my knees. I start to dig, hands hardening as I tear at the pit's stone floor.

Far and far away, carried on the wind, I hear the shrill song of harpies, the banging of drums, the march of monsters.

I punch through stone, find a pocket of empty space, and then to my horror, realize this isn't going to work. I'm not going to be able to tunnel my way out of this mess. The hole begins to fill with red-hot liquid death, lava bubbling up and forcing me back.

As it spurts and pours over the edge of the tunnel I've begun, I leap back. I can't stay here. I go to Mark's body, pick it up, and race toward the top of the pit.

The monsters are coming, creeping across the horizon like black mold. Centaurs, cyclopes, harpies, and one of the Lesser Titans, the giant Gyges, who I've battled before. Falling off the Bridge of Burnt Souls in the Cliffs of Pain didn't destroy him. I watched him vanish beneath the fiery Phlegethon, and hoped I'd never see him again.

That makes me wonder... if Gyges can live after bathing in lava, maybe I can too? Maybe it's just my old human way of thinking that warns me against it? But even if I could swim across the moat unscathed, Mark's body couldn't. He'd burn to a crisp and who wants to be resurrected like that?

I set his body down and wrap my hands around the sword hilt. I figure I'll need both blades if I'm going to take on a whole army...

"I wouldn't do that," a familiar voice says from behind me.

I whirl and see Mark standing there. I look back, and see his body where I left it. *Still dead.* I turn to face this new Mark and then I know. "You're a ghost."

Mark shrugs and gives a sad grin. "Sorry it took me so long to get here. There was this problem processing me at the main gate. The guards are used to souls arriving from the Styx-side, not from inside Tartarus."

"But Gyges' two brothers guard that entrance! Did they give you any trouble?"

"Didn't give them a chance. Made a run for it, once I got over my initial disorientation. You know, about waking up dead... *Undead.* Whatever." Mark's face suddenly goes blank and terrible, and he raises his hands in a threatening gesture as an eerie moan splits his lips. *"Woo-ooo-oooh...."*

I step back, not sure what's happening, and almost slip and fall into the pit. Mark grabs my wrist and pulls me back. He looks like his old self again. "Sorry," he says. "Ghost humor. Figured you were the only person it would work on in the Underworld."

"Ha ha," I mutter, but I'm too relieved to be mad. "You do know we're about to die, right? Well, maybe not you..."

"Them?" Mark looks over his shoulder at the advancing army. "They're not so tough."

"Yeah, because you're a ghost! It's not like they can do anything more to you."

"That's true. you know, I could get used to feeling invincible. I mean, I sort of had it when I was possessed by Ares, but that wasn't really me. I was too numb, too blissed out being possessed to worry about dying. Now..." He shrugs. "I don't really worry much about anything."

"You ran from the giants at the gate."

"Duh! Because they're giants, and old habits die hard. Besides, while they can't kill me, they can sure put me somewhere I don't want to be, like the Asphodel Meadows. Ghosts have a physical existence in the Underworld, you know. That's how I was able to grab you just now."

"So you're physical?" I reach out to touch him. I get a chill, and Mark's form wavers like a bad TV signal before bouncing back.

"Sort of," he explains. "I'm physical to other ghosts, and I guess to Gods and Titans like you. Not sure about monsters. Not really eager to find out."

"I thought you weren't worried?"

"I'm not... but I'm not here to help you fight. I'm a priest, remember? Or I was. Anyway, I came to help you pray."

I remember Hades' advice: *Pray to someone who will listen.* "To Ares?"

Mark nods.

"But won't he be a ghost too? Or an avatar?"

"His War avatar died," Mark corrects. "That freed up his last remaining earthly energy."

"Freed up? Free to go where?"

"To reunite War with the rest of his God-energy, and with his other aspects: Security, Virility, Revenge."

"So it made him more powerful?"

"No, not yet. When his last avatar died, and with no more worshippers, he passed beyond our dimension into... well, wherever Gods go when they die. We can pray him back to life, but with just the two of us, don't expect much."

"I'm not sure I expect anything anymore. The Olympians betrayed us."

Mark shrugs. "They did what they had to do to survive. Just like the Titans. Just like us." He chuckles. "Well, maybe I didn't do such a good job at that, but I'm hanging in there."

"I don't know if I can do it."

"Hope has to start somewhere," Mark says. "First hope, then belief. hope makes belief real. Belief makes the impossible possible."

"Did you learn that in priest class or is this some ghostly wisdom from beyond the grave?"

"Both. I learned it at Axios, but I didn't really believe it until now."

"OK... Hey, before, when you first ghosted in..."

"Yeah?"

"You told me not to pull the sword out of your body."

"Yep. One more blade won't win the fight."

"But the monsters..."

"I'm dead, not blind. I can see them just fine. But that sword's magic is better off in my body than in your hand—that is, if you want to resurrect me."

I think back to what Hades said and curse. "Sorry, man! I took one look at that horde and panicked. I figured I could just, um, you know... stab you again after."

Mark shakes his head. "Really?"

"Like I said, I wasn't thinking. How do you know what Hades told me? Were you eavesdropping on our conversation or what?"

"Nah. A little bird told me."

Just then, a raven squawks into view, circles once overhead, then lands on my shoulder. It's Shadow, Hannah's familiar. So she wasn't just sorry she had to leave, she made sure Mark could find me. Some of the resentment I've been wrestling with uncoils from my heart.

"Hello, Shadow."

The bird caws a greeting.

"So you speak raven now?" I ask Mark.

"I don't know. I speak familiar. I guess that's one of the perks of being a ghost."

Shadow croaks in agreement, bobbing his black head, then makes an insistent sound.

"What's he saying?" I ask Mark.

"That we better pray while we still have time."

The raven is right. The monsters are closer now. "I'm not sure how to do it, or if it's even right. I mean, I'm a Titan. Titans don't pray to Gods, do they?"

"You prayed to Cronus and the other Titans before, didn't you?"

"Yeah, but the Theocracy made everybody do that. Besides, that's when I thought I was human."

"Good point. Maybe you don't need to pray *to* Ares. Maybe you just need to pray *for* him."

"For what?"

Mark shrugs. "How about to come save your ass?"

"That's a good prayer."

"Try and make it a little more formal than that, and a lot less self-serving. Pray for Ares and what he represents: War, Security, Virility, Revenge. Pray to strengthen him, to strengthen these aspects of his divinity."

I raise an eyebrow. "You want me to pray for Virility? Are you serious?"

"No, man. Not like that! Virility's not just sex drive. It's strength, energy, aggression. Qualities every good soldier needs."

"OK, so what do I do? Just close my eyes and think good thoughts?"

Mark purses his lips. "Sure. That'd be a start..."

I shoo the raven from my shoulder and kneel to concentrate. It's hard. I don't know what to say, don't know how to make my prayer not sound selfish or stupid. I try harder, searching for the right words, the magic words.

Nothing happens.

"It's not working," I grumble.

Mark sighs. "We're trying to bring a God back to life and have been at it for what? Five minutes? And already you're complaining?"

I look across the moat to the monster army. "I know, but it's not like we have a lot of time! Those bastards won't wait for us to get the words right."

"It's not a matter of words," Mark says. "Gods don't care about words, not in the way you think. They only care about *intent*. The words merely give shape to your intentions; they help channel the energy. If your energy, your intent, line up with a God's, that's when the channel opens, not before. So forget about saying the perfect prayer and start *feeling* it."

"You mean start feeling war?"

Mark nods. "Yeah, and the rest. Chant them if it's easier: *War, Security, Virility, Revenge*. Imagine yourself attaining peak form in each."

"OK, I can do that. Then what?"

"When you're really feeling it, that's when you give your feelings a name: *Ares*."

"Damn, man! That makes sense. Can I tell you something?"

The cry of harpies shrills the air. "Sure, if you hurry."

"I'm sorry you died, but I'm really glad you're here... I hope you know what I mean. I couldn't have done this without you."

He laughs. "What? You mean pray?"

"No, man. Any of it."

"Bring me back to life, save my sister, and we'll call it even, all right?"

"You got it."

"Good. Now let's get back to prayer."

I pray smarter this time, not harder. I see myself fighting, winning, avenging, until the cities burn and the streets run red with blood.

I see myself stand over the bodies of my enemies, secure at last.

I see myself with Lucy, with Hannah, virile in my lovemaking. I hear their cries of pleasure mingled with my own, our sounds rising, surging with the cheers of the people, of humanity freed from bondage.

I see it all, and I give it a name: "Ares!" It comes out as a harsh whisper, so I say it again, louder, again and again until it becomes a shout, a prayer, a purpose: "ARES!"

Mark shouts the War God's name too.

For a moment, I think nothing's going to happen. That we failed again, but I push that thought aside and hold on to hope.

The air ripples, becomes a shimmering haze, a gasoline sheen. "ARES!" we shout again. "WE BELIEVE!"

The haze coalesces into a glowing humanoid shape. It has no face, its body no detail, but when I stare at it, I see our old gym teacher, Mr. Cross, standing there, his eyes red-gold. It's the disguise Ares used to train me back at the Academy, and to hide from his enemies. I know it's not really Mr. Cross here, but it's how I see Ares, how I know him.

"Does he look like Mr. Cross to you?" I ask Mark.

"No. He looks like me."

"Maybe we're seeing him how we think of him. I guess since you were his vessel, it makes sense for you to see him as you."

"Yeah," Mark says. "I guess we better talk to him."

But before we can, Ares walks past us, toward the moat.

I run after him. "Ares? Hey, wait up!"

"The time for waiting is done," the War God says in that gruff voice I know so well, the voice from class that told me to climb, to fight, to never surrender. "Now is the time to act," he says, "my energy is limited. I cannot give you War, nor Virility, nor Revenge."

"Then what can you give us?"

He snorts. "A miracle." The War God walks to the moat, then into it. He doesn't sink, just stands there, arms outstretched, facing downriver.

"What's he doing?" I ask Mark.

"Giving us what he can: Security."

"How do you know that?"

Mark shrugs. "Process of elimination. Security is the only aspect he didn't mention."

"What's he saying? And who is he talking to? Hades?"

"No, not Hades."

"Then who?"

Mark doesn't answer. He doesn't need to. I can see who Ares is talking to. There's a long, gondola-like boat poling down the river. A boat adorned with bones, with skulls.

Charon's boat.

Charon, Ferryman of the Dead, Deliverer of Souls. His dried, desiccated husk stands at the boat's rear. The living mummy's dark, empty eyes lock on mine. The bearded, silent boatman has never been a more welcome sight and I let out a cheer.

We're going to do it.

We're going to escape.

3

NO PRAYER IS ENOUGH

The boat glides up just as the monster army reaches the opposite shore. Gyges strides to the molten edge. He's a fifty-foot combination of man and beast, towering over the centaurs and cyclopes behind him. Gyges has fifty heads and a hundred arms, each uglier than the last. Not all his heads are human, or even human-ish. Some are reptilian, some bird-like, some insect, while others are bestial: lions, bears, wolves. They glare out in every possible direction. Likewise, not all the giant's arms are human either. Some are tentacles, and still others are the pincers of crabs.

But the "face" that draws the eye is the central one in Gyges' torso. It's spider-like, with eight black eyes surrounding a fanged and suckered mouth. Beneath that, the Titan's lower-half descends into the dark-furred haunches of a goat, yet his black taloned feet are those of an eagle.

For all his terrible might, I know Gyges can be hurt. His body is covered in blisters and scabs from his fall into the Phlegethon. Now that Hades is free, I know Gyges can be killed.

"Little brother!" Gyges calls. "Where are you going?" His inhuman heads growl, roar, and shriek their own taunts, their own challenges.

I ignore them all and set Mark's body into the bottom of Charon's boat. Mark's ghost climbs aboard, then Shadow lands on Charon's shoulder with a squawk. The bearded mummy holds out a skeletal hand to me, palm up.

"I don't have any drachmas or diamonds to pay you," I tell the bearded mummy.

Charon leans forward, and takes my hand in his. The skin is leathery, paper-thin and shriveled. The bony fingers grip my hand with surprising strength. At first I think he's mad, then I realize he's helping me into his boat.

"Thanks," I say.

Charon stares at me, then points to Ares.

I turn to the War God, still standing over the lava. "Ares? You coming?"

He turns to me, jaw set in a grim line. "No, I have given you Security, now you must give me War, Virility, Revenge."

"What do you mean? Our prayers weren't enough?"

"No prayer is ever enough. Action makes prayer reality. Give me my sword."

"Your sword?" I stare down at the golden blade sticking out of Mark's ribs, then realize he means its twin, the sword at my side. "I can only give you the one. Mark needs the other."

"I know. One is all I need against this scum."

"You got it." I unsheath the blade and hand it to Ares. "I admire your confidence, but you sure you're up for this? I mean, you're not at full-strength..."

He grips the sword, knuckles popping. "Fighting gives me energy. War is its own prayer. And revenge."

I don't ask him about virility.

"Belief does not just come from those who love you," Ares says, "but from those who fear you."

"And you're going to make them fear you?"

The War God smirks. "It's what I do best. Now go! I'll catch up with you later."

Charon dips his pole into the flaming river, pushing us off from the island's shore and away from the coming battle. If the bearded mummy is worried, he doesn't show it.

Gyges does not look pleased. "Only cowards run!" he taunts. "You won't get far, little brother. I will find you! I will find you, and then we will finish our fight..." The Titan gestures to some of his troops to pursue us: Captain Nessus leads a squad of centaurs along the shoreline, while a flock of harpies takes wing behind us.

And Ares, the God of War reborn, stalks across the lava into battle. He doesn't look back.

"He'll be all right," Mark says. "Ares is tough. I know better than anyone."

I don't answer, just watch the fight. Ares slices through first one cyclops, then another. Getting faster, getting stronger. He needs blood and battle. He needs it to live. But what about me? What do I need?

Part of me wants to be back there, fighting beside him, and part of me wants to be far away. At peace. One with the Earth. That's what I'm fighting for. The chance to be free, or at least to have that choice. For everyone to have it, because everyone deserves it: Mark, Lucy, Hannah. *Me.*

The rage of monsters jolts me out of my thoughts. They're closer now, in danger of catching up, and then I see why.

Mark is flipping them off.

"What the hell, man? What are you doing?"

He glares at the onrushing creatures defiantly. "What's it look like? I'm giving them the finger."

"I know you're new to this ghost thing, but you know they can see you, right?"

"Sure, that's why I'm doing it."

That doesn't sound like Mark at all, and I wonder how much being possessed by Ares may have changed him. Being possessed— or being dead.

I duck as a volley of spears come sailing at us. Harpies shrill overhead, hurtling down, talons poised to tear us apart.

Mark doesn't move. Charon doesn't react, though he's undead, so I suppose he doesn't have anything to fear either.

The spears hit an invisible shield around our boat and bounce harmlessly into the lava. The harpies bounce too, though the sharp crack of bone tells me the impact wasn't so harmless to them.

Two of the vulture-women fall into the fiery river, black feathers bursting into flame, the death-shriek short as they sink beneath the burning ooze.

I stand up. "That was crazy! How did you know about the shield?"

"Hannah told us, remember?"

"Oh, yeah... when we ran into the river monster in the Pillars of Ash. I forgot."

"You've got a lot on your mind. I forgot too."

"Then how did you know?"

Mark jerks a thumb at the boatman. "Charon reminded me."

"But his telepathy only works on Hannah or..." I stop myself, feeling stupid.

"You can say it: *with the dead*. So I guess be glad I'm a ghost so I can translate for him. It's bound to come in handy."

"I'll never be glad you're dead."

"Me either," Mark says, "but I'm making the best of it. No reason not to. Anyway, once I knew you'd be safe, I figured I could mess with our pursuers. That's less spears to worry about, and two less harpies. Not bad for one middle finger."

"Not bad," I agree. "So we're safe—as long as we stay in the boat. And after?"

Mark shrugs. "That's when the fun begins."

"Murder Town?"

"Murder Town," Mark repeats. "I was kind of hoping we could avoid that place while we were down here."

I shake my head. "Damn! Seems like every place Hannah told us about, we're gonna see."

"All the horrible places. I don't think Elysium or the Fortunate Isles are in the cards."

"No, I suppose not."

Mark watches the monsters trailing behind us, getting smaller as the boat picks up speed. I'm not sure how we're doing that; Charon isn't poling any faster. He just keeps creaking along, leathery flesh tight against his bones.

"Magic," Mark explains, noticing my interest in our sudden burst of speed. "You want me to translate how he does it?"

"No."

Mark nods. "It's complicated anyway. You know, you wouldn't think it to look at the guy, but Charon's quite a talker—if you can hear him."

The living mummy's neck bones crack at the sound of his name, the skull-like visage turning to stare at us through empty eye sockets. His expression is unchanging, as unreadable as always.

Mark cocks his head, listening to words I cannot hear. "Charon says he's going to try to give those bastards the slip."

"Seriously? Is that how he talks?"

"I'm paraphrasing," Mark says. "Just be glad I'm not doing the accent."

I smile, glad Mark hasn't lost his sense of humor along with his life. Charon returns his attention to the river. If he's offended, he doesn't show it.

Mark points to a modern backpack in the prow of the ship, one I hadn't paid attention to before.

"What's in the bag?"

"Open it."

I do, and find it full of water bottles and packaged food from Earth.

"It's one of Hannah's stashes," Mark explains. "She told Charon where to find it. Go on, eat. Just save some for me. I'll need it after I'm human again."

I tear into an energy bar and down a bottle of water, then on a full belly, take stock of our remaining supplies. "We should be good, supply-wise. Shouldn't have to ration much. We won't be down here long."

Mark nods. "It already feels like forever."

"I know what you mean."

"Not quite, you don't." He looks down, down at his corpse—the corpse with the sword sticking out of it, rocking gently in the bottom of the boat. "Time is different for the dead."

I clear my throat. "I—um, I'm going to petition Hades, you know. On your behalf. To go to Elysium or the Fortunate Isles. Whatever's best. There's no way I'm letting you spend your afterlife in the Asphodel Meadows."

Mark turns to me. "I don't intend to stay a ghost, Andrus."

"I know, I'm just saying, after you're human again, and after you die for keeps a long time from now. I'm going to make sure you get the best deal. A ghost-mansion, hot ghost-babes..."

He looks at me funny.

"What? You'll be dead! Plenty of time to get your game on."

He cracks a grin. "I don't need all that."

"OK. What about ghost-books? A great big library you can study forever. All the knowledge in the world and the time to take it in."

Mark nods, considering this. "Don't get me wrong. That all sounds great—even the babes—but I'm not sure that's how it works. So thanks..."

"But no thanks?"

"I didn't say that! It's not like I'm going to say no to your petition... hell, to any of it... but I want to earn it on my own if I can. *Heroes do, dreamers dream.* The one thing I learned living in Loserville is you gotta work to get out. You've got to work hard. You find your way and you just keep going till you're gone."

"You're already a hero, Mark."

He looks at the creatures on our tail, distant but tenacious. "Yeah, a dead one."

"Maybe those are the best kind."

He raises an eyebrow. "How you figure?"

I shrug. "Nobody can take your glory from you. That's the one thing you take with you when you die: *who you are.*"

"Glory," Mark muses. "Never thought I'd have any. Not this kind, anyway. It feels..."

"Good?"

"No, incomplete. Like my life."

"We'll win this," I tell him. "We'll bring you back to life, and rescue Lucy."

Mark nods. "I know. I know we will. We don't have a choice."

He's right. We lapse into silence as the boat sails on. Behind us, the centaurs and harpies follow.

4

WITH ANY LUCK

The Phlegethon flows, hot and sulfurous. Winding through Tartarus like a crimson snake. The smoke, the fumes are thicker here, so toxic it takes a coughing fit for my inhuman lungs to adjust.

We lost the monsters some time ago, taking a detour when the river forked. A detour that will lead them—and us—away from Murder Town, but one which Charon assures us won't cost much time.

He tells Mark—and Mark translates to me—that his boat's magic can manipulate our position in the river to make us appear anywhere, even on another river totally unconnected to this one. That's how he gets around Tartarus, ferrying souls and whatever else he does. The only problem is it takes time, but the time we spend now buys time later. Charon's making it look like we're heading for the Styx, for the Pillars of Ash and beyond, back the way we came to Earth.

The hope is the monsters will keep going in that direction while we sneak back to Murder Town. Charon thinks they'll figure it out eventually and show up there, but with any luck, Mark will be alive and we'll be long gone by then...

With any luck.

I decide to send Shadow ahead, to scout out the area and make sure there isn't any obvious trap or signs of monster activity. Mark translates to the raven for me and it flies off.

"He'll either meet us downriver with a warning or find us when we get to the city." Mark says. "It's a good idea to scout ahead to see stuff inside the city—stuff away from the river Charon can't see—but that bird is the only one who can guide us to Dr. Herophilos…"

"We'll be fine," I assure him. "You know, it's funny…"

"What is?"

"I used to be such a loner. I had my family, my sports, my hobbies. I had friends, of course, but not real friends. I always held them at arm's length… afraid to let them get too close."

Mark doesn't reply. "You beat me there, man. I didn't have any, except my sister. When you're a smart kid in Loserville, it's hard to make friends. Everyone wants to tear you down, tell you to stop acting better than them. Especially when you have a scholarship to Axios. But you can't help the way you are. Sure, you can hide it, but you can't stop, and you only kill yourself when you try."

"You really had it coming and going. I knew about the kids at school, of course—how they treated you. But I never knew what it was like for you back home. I figured you'd be a hero there. Someone to look up to."

"It's hard to look up to someone when you've always got your head down. A lot of folks are afraid to look up. Afraid to get hope. Because when you've got nothing, hope can be a poison. Better to keep your head down if you want to survive."

"But you wanted to do more than that."

"I had to," he says. "I saw a chance and I took it. I rolled the dice and it got me killed."

"It got you more than that."

Mark sighs. "Yeah, you're right. It got my mom zombified and my sister hurt, dead, or who knows what. That's the truth."

"That's not all of it. Your future's still being written. You were a hero in life, and you're a hero in death. You're also my best friend."

"Ha! I'm your only friend."

"That just makes it easier to narrow down who the best one is."

"I guess it does," Mark admits. "You're my best friend too. Just promise me one thing, all right? Well, one more thing."

"Sure, buddy. What's that?"

"Don't get me killed twice."

5

SOON

MURDER TOWN IS CRUEL, an impossible city of jagged lines and jagged souls, home to ghosts of the damned and depraved. But theirs is damnation by choice, a surrender to sadism and savagery for the pleasures of control—or being out of it.

I wonder how any soul can live here, but when you can't die, when your actions have no lasting consequences, maybe that's the appeal. If you're the killer, you never run out of victims—or, if you're the victim, you never run out of lives.

Charon guides us toward our violent destination. Murder Town, a symbol of death to others, a symbol of life for us. The boat glides down the Acheron, the River of Woe, a river of blood that keeps the evil and those obsessed with evil away from the rest of Tartarus.

Which is weird... I'm not sure how we got here. One minute, we're cruising the Phlegethon, plowing through bubbling lava with the monster army in pursuit along the shore. The next, we're here, on the Acheron, and the change was so gradual, I didn't even notice until I saw the gleaming black spires of Murder Town pierce the horizon.

I turn to Charon to ask him, then remember I won't hear him anyway, so I ask Mark to ask the ferryman for me.

"You know he's not deaf, right?" Mark teases, but asks him anyway.

Charon shrugs, then gestures at the hull, his finger bones clacking.

"What'd he say?" I ask.

"He said, 'Magic.'"

"Right." I shake my head. "Of course. Magic's the answer for everything down here."

Mark doesn't reply, and if Charon does, I don't hear it.

"What about Gyges and the army chasing us?" This time, I ask Charon directly. "They can't teleport or whatever like we did, can they?"

Charon shakes his head.

"So how much time until they catch up?"

The ferryman shrugs.

Mark says, "He's not sure. They have to know where we're going first."

"And do they?"

Charon cranes his neck toward the cavernous ceiling with its gems for stars, as if sensing something.

"Well?" I ask.

"Hang on," Mark says. "He's checking. He knows everything that happens along the rivers of the underworld."

"He knows or has to specifically check? There's a big difference."

Charon finishes and turns his head toward us. Mark listens to the boatman's telepathic message, then relays it to me: "He says his relationship with the rivers is more complicated than that, so the answer is yes, he knows everything, but only eventually. He has to specifically check for new events, and this takes time, and if he's busy or doesn't know what to look for, it can take a while."

"And the answer to my first question?"

Mark smiles. "Oh, that? No, man. On that, we're good. All good. *So good.* They're not heading this way at all."

"So we've got time, then? To save you?"

"Dude, I'm not a princess locked in a tower. I don't need 'saving,' I just need to be brought back to life."

I nod. "Yeah, sorry. I know. I just meant..." I let the words trail off. They can't lead anywhere good. Then a thought occurs to me, and I'm glad to change the subject, glad to fill the awkward silence that stretches between us. "Didn't Hannah say only evil ghosts could cross the Acheron? How are you going to get across the river?"

Mark pats the skull and bone encrusted side of the boat. "No worries. Charon can deliver souls anywhere."

"OK, great. So nothing to worry about."

"Nope. We'll have no problem getting into Murder Town... it's getting back out that presents a problem."

Charon interrupts by reaching into his robe and pulling out the diamond I gave him earlier to buy our passage into the underworld.

I hesitate, not sure what's expected of me.

"Go on," Mark says. "Take it. Charon says when we need a ride out, toss the diamond in the river and he'll pick us up."

I take the gem, asking, "How long will it take for Charon to show up? We might be in a hurry."

The boatman shrugs.

"What's that supposed to mean?" I ask Mark.

"Soon."

"Soon? That's not a really precise measurement of time. What are we talking about? Five minutes? Ten? An hour?"

Mark laughs. "Soon means soon. Ghosts and immortals don't like to think of time in mortal terms."

"Yeah? Well, I do."

"Time doesn't flow the same in Tartarus, Andrus. You know that. So 'soon' means 'as fast as he can,' but his perception of fast and yours might differ."

"By a little or a lot?"

"By however much it does," Mark explains. "Believe me, Charon knows how urgent our request is."

The living mummy bows slightly, bones creaking under his leathery flesh.

"He'll be there," Mark insists. "We can trust him. And if we can't stay put, all we have to do is stay near the river. He'll find us."

I look into Charon's empty eye sockets, his blank, bony expression as ghoulishly neutral as ever. Something passes between us, something I can't hear, but something I can sense, or think I can. It feels like trust. Charon hasn't let us down yet. I give the bearded mummy a nod, and he nods back.

"Thanks," I tell him, but the boatman just points. I follow the direction of his robed arm to the broken bridge coming up. The same stone bridge I saw when we came close to Murder Town before. The bridge where the madmen "fished" for victims in the blood-water with hangman's nooses. Victims they would lasso and strangle, leaving them to twist and kick in the hellish wind.

There are no ghosts here now. No killers or victims. Just ropes lashed to spiked iron posts in the bridge's railing high above.

"There's no dock," Mark says. "We're gonna have to climb if we want to get into the city."

"Seriously? I don't want to touch those death ropes!"

"And I don't want to be dead, but here we are... Anyway, I thought climbing was your thing. It'll be just like gym class. If you need extra motivation, just pretend Mr. Cross is yelling at you. Ready?"

"No."

"Too bad."

"Wait! How are we supposed to get your body up there?"

"Shit!" Mark curses. "I forgot about that."

"Can you possess it?"

"How? It's dead."

"I don't know, but you gotta try!"

Mark's ghost form shimmers and shifts, becoming smoke-like, funneling through the open mouth of his corpse. But the body doesn't move. The bridge gets closer.

"Mark?" I say, shaking him by the shoulders. "Come on, man! You can do this."

The eyelids creep open, and a low moan comes from Mark's

mouth. He looks like a zombie. Like how his mom looked when we found her hanging in their shack.

"Quit fooling around," I tell him. "Get up!"

"Can't... hurts..."

"You're dead. You can't feel anything! Just move your ass or we're not going to make it."

Zombie Mark raises a hand. I grab it and pull him to his feet.

"*Hurts!*" Mark repeats. "*Can't stay in... long...*"

"You don't need to. Just long enough to get up that rope. OK?"

Mark nods, the same stiff-necked kind Charon gives, with the same weary crunching of bone. My friend's face is slack-jawed, expressionless, the eyes dull and staring, the skin drawn and bloodless. But there is strength in Mark's grip, and it will have to be enough.

"Ready? We're going in three... two... one!"

Mark jumps first, catching a rope, holding tight, and I jump too. The rope is covered in dried blood that flakes off under my fingers. I look down and see Charon's living dead face staring back at us, then his boat sails from view under the bridge.

We haul ourselves up.

Up, into Murder Town.

6

STREETS OF BLOOD

We pull ourselves over the stone railing. The bridge is empty, and I'm grateful. Grateful we made it, and glad there were no crazed ghosts waiting to greet us. "So this is it," I say. "Murder Town."

Mark groans in reply, then collapses, his body crumpling in on itself as his ghost shakes free.

"You all right?" I ask, going to steady him, but I forget he's a ghost again. My hands pass right through, chilling me, and causing his outline to waver.

Mark shakes his head. "Gimme a minute… That was hard… Hard and awful to be trapped inside myself, dead like that… I can't… can't even…"

I look from him to his corpse. "I'm sorry. It was the only way."

He nods and waves me off. "I get it… I do, just gimme a minute… gotta regain my strength."

I walk to the other side of the bridge, just in time to see Charon drifting away, but not just drifting. Fading. I rub my eyes and when I look again, the river's there, but the ferryman is gone.

Magic.

I pat my pocket to make sure the diamond is still there. It is. It's safe, even if we aren't.

We can do this, I tell myself. *I can do this.* Mark will be alive again, and everything will be fine... Well, not fine. Back to normal. Except 'normal' doesn't exist for me anymore. For any of us.

I think back to what Hannah told me the last time we were here. 'We all kill,' she'd told me. 'You, me, Ares... Every God and Titan kills. It's the reason why you kill that matters.' Maybe... maybe she's right. Maybe morality is different for creatures like us. Less fixed, more situational.

'We all have lines,' Hannah had warned. 'Lines we dare not cross, lines we think will break us... until we realize they won't, that life goes on, so we draw new ones.'

What lines have I drawn since she spoke those words to me? What lines will I draw before this journey is over?

"Hey," Mark says at my side. He seems better now, stronger.

I don't answer right away. I watch the Acheron. The crimson river flows, an open wound across the land. I find myself wishing we were on it, that Mark was alive, that we were in Charon's boat sailing far away from here. But to where? To an uncomplicated past before all this pain or to an uncertain future with Cronus at the end?

No, not just with Cronus at the end—with me, and who I'll become... or what.

"Andrus?" Mark asks. "You all right?"

"Yeah." I tear my gaze away from the river's bloody depths. "What do you think happened to Shadow? Wasn't he supposed to meet us?"

Mark nods. "Yeah. Either he's following up on a lead, or..." He lets the sentence drift off.

"You don't think he's dead, do you?"

Mark shrugs. "I hope not, but this is Murder Town. Maybe you shouldn't have sent him ahead."

"Maybe you're right."

"Don't forget my body." Mark points to his corpse, lying cold and lifeless on the cobblestones. "We're going to need that."

I pick it up, slinging the dead weight over my shoulder. As we come off the bridge, we run into a group of ghostly "fishermen" like the ones we saw the first time we passed the city. Each of them holds a noose. They stare at us, and I force a smile and pat Mark's corpse on the leg.

"Good fishing today," I say as we walk past. "The bodies are really biting!"

∼

THE AIR REEKS OF COPPER. Faint screams and laughter carry on the wind along with the smell. It's no surprise. Murder Town looks exactly how I think it should. It's a nightmare city of sharp angles where the buildings look like knives, broken skulls, and other sharp and nasty things. Despite that, the place has a strange and terrible beauty, the kind you could get lost in—and we do.

It's not like we want to stop and ask anyone for directions. The ghosts who dwell here either aren't friendly, or else they're *too friendly*. Several times, we have to rebuff the advances of ghosts who want to become our victims, or who want us to become theirs. It's all a game to them, some sick, never-ending game, but so far, no one's tried to force us to play...

We know enough to avoid the dark alleys—Murder Town seems to be riddled with them, and they are filled with strange shapes—sinister shadows that move and beckon.

The main street—Mercy Street—seems safe enough. There seems to be some kind of understanding that as long as you're on it, you're either coming from or on your way to a game. We do get a few long, hungry looks and the occasional cry of "Fresh meat!" but no one attacks us, nor do we pick up any strange pursuit—at least none we can see.

In some ways, it's a lot like walking through the streets of Othrys back home with people on their way to work or going home. Only here, that "work" is murder, and I don't even want to guess what home is like...

We pass a hunchbacked street vendor selling rats on a stick, only these vermin aren't cooked. They're not even dead! Just wriggling in pain.

"This place is horrible," I whisper.

"No doubt," Mark replies. "Just be glad he's only selling rats!"

"Wait, what else would he be..." The sound of a crying baby makes me stop. I jerk my head around, but the hunchback is only impaling another rat to hang with the rest of his wares. The sound of the baby came from somewhere else, a mother and child passing us, perhaps, or a sound from one of the dingy, smoke-damaged apartments looming above.

I hurry to catch up to Mark who has stopped to ask a ghost for directions. The ghost is a plain-looking girl in a wine-colored dress. She appears nervous, wide eyes peering out from a long face. Under her arm she carries a wicker basket, the kind used for picnics, and its contents are covered by a red and white checkerboard cloth. The girl has one arm stuck through the basket's looped handle while both hands smooth and tug the wrinkles from her dress. It's almost charming, a demure gesture in this monstrous place.

As I get closer, I realize she's not smoothing out the material, she's wiping something off her hands. That something is blood. And as she does it, the motion causes her basket to tip forward, spilling its ghoulish contents into the street.

Parts.

Body parts.

Parts of children: infants.

She kneels to scoop up her terrible treasures, muttering darkly.

Mark turns as I approach. "Hey, so I got directions."

The strange girl looks up at me. "It's not far," she says in a high, thin voice. "Nothing's too far here..."

"Thanks," I say, more out of politeness than wanting to talk to her.

"Do you want to come to a picnic?" the girl asks. "I'm having a picnic. I have one everyday, but no one ever comes, and I don't know why. I ask and ask, and now I'm asking you."

I adjust Mark's corpse on my shoulder. "Um, no. We can't. We're busy, see? Already got a body of our own. Big plans. You know how it is."

"Yeah," Mark adds. "Thanks for the directions."

She gives us a funny look, eyes wide with the wisdom of the mad. "Everyone wants to go somewhere until they realize there's no place to go," she says. "No place but here." She taps the side of her forehead. "It's the only safe spot left."

"OK. Well, we better get going. Right, Mark?"

The girl mumbles something in reply as we hurry away. When I glance back, she's busy on her hands and knees picking up the demented pieces of her picnic.

My stomach coils into knots and I have to swallow hard not to vomit. "Seriously, Mark? Of all the people you had to ask, you had to pick Abortion Annie?"

"I didn't pick her," he protests. "She picked me."

"What do you mean?"

"She stopped and asked if I wanted to go on a picnic. So I used the opportunity to ask for directions. Besides, it's not like any of the other people would have been any better."

I want to argue, but realize Mark is right. We can't be picky. We can't waste time. "So where is it?"

"This way," he replies.

Naturally, the doctor's office is down an alley—a dark one.

7
DEAD END

The sign over the alley reads SCALPEL CLOSE. A "close" is another name for a dead end, so I'm not sure if whoever named it was trying to be funny, warn people, or both.

Mark's a ghost and doesn't need to breathe, but I see him take a deep and completely unnecessary breath anyway.

"Does that help?" I ask.

Mark looks confused for a moment, then grins. "Force of habit, I guess. And you know what? It kind of does! Like, I know I'm not really taking a deep breath, but it focuses my spirit energy pretty much the same way as if I had. What about you? You need to take a moment before we go in?"

"Only to draw my sword." I tug the magic blade free of its scabbard. The fiery golden glow lights up the alley.

"It'll just be ghosts," Mark says. "If there's even anything in there. It's not like Gyges or a bunch of centaurs could fit. The alley's too narrow."

"I know... But I'd rather be ready for anything." I step over a rancid puddle, thrusting my blade forward to light the way.

Scalpel Close is long and narrow, wet and dripping not just with moisture, but with other fluids as well. There are a variety of doctor's offices and medical supply companies wedged in here, each more grim and foreboding than the last. Bloodcurdling screams come from behind closed doors. The alley ends in a padlocked metal door with a sign that reads, MURDER TOWN ASYLUM FOR THE ETERNALLY INSANE.

Cheery.

On closer inspection, I notice both the door and the padlock are covered in mystic symbols—presumably to keep the most violent, insane ghosts trapped inside.

"Are you sure this is it?" I ask Mark. "I didn't think Herophilos was that kind of doctor."

"He isn't," a voice says from behind us.

I just about jump out of my skin, but that's hard to do when I'm carrying a dead body, so I turn around as fast as I can.

There's a man—or rather, the ghost of a man—standing in the alley. He's in his fifties, sharp-featured, with a long face and olive-skin. He wears a long blue toga trimmed in gold.

"Dr. Herophilos!" I blurt. "We've been looking for you!"

"I know," he says, "Shadow told me to expect you. He also informed me of the unusual nature of your visit. I'd put that sword away, if I were you. It's only going to draw attention—the wrong kind."

I sheathe my sword and shift Mark's body to my other shoulder. "Is there any other kind here?"

"Some trouble is worse than others."

"Can you help us? We need—" Mark begins, but the doctor cuts him off.

"Not here. In a town full of ghosts, the walls have ears, among other things..." Herophilos casts a backward glance over his shoulder. "Quickly now! Come to my office." He leads us from the eternal asylum, back up the alley to one of the doors we passed.

"But there's no sign," Mark protests. "How is anyone supposed to find you?"

Herophilos smirks. "They're not. My work is too important to be bothered by walk-ins." He works a key in the lock and pulls the door back to let us in. The doctor looks up and down the alley, then ducks inside and locks the door. I notice there are runes on his lock and key similar to the ones I saw on the asylum.

I look around the vacant reception area: a nurse's desk, some chairs, a large plant for color. "Is there someplace we can…"

"Put the body?" Herophilos answers for me. "Yes, in the examination room. This way, gentlemen, this way…" He takes us down a hallway covered in a mural showing what looks to be a younger version of himself conducting prison experiments.

"My glory days," Herophilos says with a dismissive wave of his hand. "I thought I knew the mysteries of life then, but it was only through death that I learned its true secrets…"

The mural proudly show him dissecting living victims in the legendary experiments that gained him his fame—and his infamy—all those centuries ago. I try to remind myself that without his work, advances in western medicine would have been delayed by hundreds of years.

"Was it worth it?" I ask.

"My work?" Herophilos says with a start. "Of course! Think of what the world gained."

"I was thinking of what you lost."

He snorts as if I'm the madman. "The end justifies the means. You're a Titan… if you don't understand that by now, you will… Sooner than you think."

"Andrus," Mark intervenes, "this isn't the time or the place to question the doctor's choices. Right or wrong, they made him the man he is today, and he's the only man who can help us."

"You're right," I say. "I apologize, doctor."

"It's nothing I haven't heard before." Herophilos unlocks a door at the end of the hall. It opens to reveal a surprisingly modern examination room—shiny, neat, orderly—not the blood-soaked butcher's shop I expected.

"I try to keep up on the latest advances in comfort and design," he explains, motioning for me to set Mark's body down on the exam table. "Hannah has been helpful in that regard, summoning me to Earth not just to assist her, but to aid my experiments."

There are a variety of specimens sealed in jars of amber fluid. Some recognizable, some not, and some still moving...

I lay Mark's body on the padded vinyl table and step back. Leaning against the counter, I rub my shoulder and close my eyes, smelling the antiseptic quality of the room. For a moment—just one—I imagine none of this is real, that everything's normal and I'm back home in Othrys with my family. We're at my doctor's office waiting for a checkup, or maybe one of my sports injuries.

But that life is dead and gone, as dead as Mark, and I am here, in Murder Town. In the office of a mad doctor, a ghost doctor, yet one who has helped us before, and who can help us now.

With a sigh—half in relief, half in resignation—I open my eyes. "What do we have to do?"

Dr. Herophilos smiles.

8

LIFE IS PAIN

The procedure to bring Mark back to life isn't as hard as I thought... at least not the way Dr. Herophilos explains it. All we have to do is get Mark's ghost to possess Mark's body... and stay.

"We already tried that," I say.

Mark nods. "It hurt. It hurts to be dead, trapped inside myself, rotting like that."

Herophilos shrugs. "Life is pain... all life, especially when it is unnatural. The fact you were able to possess your corpse at all proves there is magic in it. But is it enough?"

"Hades said there was," Mark insists.

"No doubt there was—when Hades told you. Unfortunately, you used up some of that magic when you possessed the body."

Mark and I exchange a worried look.

"There is a way," the doctor continues, "to restore the magic to its previous levels."

"How?" I ask, and Mark adds, "Just tell us what we have to do."

"Have you ever heard the expression, 'your body is a temple'?" Herophilos asks.

"Sure," I say, "but what does that have to do with—"

"No, wait. I get it." Mark says. "At least, I think I do."

The doctor raises a gray furred brow and gives him an expectant look, like a teacher who has just called on a child.

"Ares," Mark says. "He possessed my body before, he was in it when I died. The magic in me is his—both from the possession and his blade."

"So what are you saying?" I ask.

"That I should invite Ares to possess me again, and make my body his temple."

"There is one more thing you need to do," Herophilos says. "To do that, to invest the act with the maximum amount of magic—the maximum amount of psychic bonding to be precise—you need to commit to that for life. And what does every temple require?"

"A priest," Mark says.

Herophilos nods. "Precisely. Is that a commitment you feel comfortable with?"

Mark frowns, looking thoughtful. Finally, he says, "Well, I am a priest, and I am between deities. Every priest needs a God. I never thought mine would be one of war."

"The decision is entirely up to you," Herophilos says. "Are you sure?"

"I am," Mark says. "What do I need to do?"

"Pray to Ares. Make your bargain, state your devotion. Andrus and I will give you some privacy. There are some materials we need to gather for the ritual, and I need to prepare myself to conduct it."

"You sure?" I ask Mark. "Maybe there's another way."

"If there is, we don't have time to find it. Go on, get the stuff the doctor needs. I've got some serious praying to do."

Herophilos and I leave Mark to his task, shutting the exam room door behind us. He leads me to reception, where he goes behind the nurse's desk and writes me a shopping list. Despite the modernity of the exam room, he uses parchment and a quill and ink pot to make out the list.

"You're sure this is going to work?" I ask him.

The doctor looks up from his list, annoyed. "I healed your friend in life, I can heal him in death."

"Yeah, but this isn't..."

"Isn't what?"

I shrug. "I don't know. It isn't medicine, it isn't science."

"Isn't it?" Herophilos asks.

"I just thought it would be... different, that's all."

The ghost snorts and returns to his list-making. "When I was a young man, I thought very much as you. That everything must be the way I thought it should be, the way I was told it would be by the men who came before me... Then I opened my first living patient and..." Herophilos' eyes take on a wistful, dream-like expression.

"And?" I prompt.

"*Magic!*" he says. "Beneath all the skin and blood and bone, beyond what the eyes can see, there is what the soul can know. There's magic in us—in all of us! It's how we go on, why we come to Tartarus, and why your friend can return to Earth." He hands me the list. "Bring me everything exactly as I have written. No substitutions, no compromises. Understood?"

I read it over. It's a long list with a lot of weird items I don't recognize. "What's all this stuff?"

"Alchemical supplies. I have all the surgical requirements in stock, but obviously, there's a bit more to this operation than that."

"Operation? You called it a ritual earlier."

The doctor shrugs. "It's both. Normally, I would agree the terms aren't interchangeable, but in this case—*this very special case*—they are indeed one and the same."

I don't like the sound of that. "OK, but won't I need money or..."

Herophilos reaches into the desk drawer and tosses me a jingling sack of coins. "Take this, and hurry. Your friend doesn't have much time."

The sack is stained red at the bottom. "You didn't mention that before."

"Never upset a patient before the procedure, Andrus. It taints the results."

9

MERCY STREET

HEROPHILOS GIVES DIRECTIONS to where the alchemy shop is located and advises me to stay on the main road. I was right that nothing bad can happen on Mercy Street. It's a safe zone, as are all the shops and public spaces along it—but not the alleys.

Never the alleys.

All the killers and victims agree Mercy Street must remain free of violence. Those who violate the rule—or refuse to agree to it in the first place—are punished by being locked in the asylum. *Forever.*

Even in Murder Town, the Asylum for the Eternally Insane has a sinister reputation. A reputation so unsettling that even the worst maniacs and madmen think twice about breaking the law.

Herophilos didn't have time to answer all my questions, and part of me is glad. I'm not sure I want to know.

I step out into Scalpel Close, into the hot, stinking musk of Murder Town. I remember Herophilos' warning not to use my magic sword to light the way, but when my boots squish into a pothole filled with organs, I draw the glowing blade anyway. I kick off the worst off the human muck clinging to my boots, then hurry down the alley. Past the marked and unmarked doors. Past the screams and shouts and whimpers coming from behind them. Only when I'm near the end do I sheathe my sword, then casually walk into Mercy Street.

I let the crowd carry me toward the Market District. I try not to make eye contact with anyone, try not to bump into any ghosts. If I do, I'll pass right through them, and they'll know I'm not dead. I don't need that kind of attention.

The alchemy shop borders a public park. There's a guillotine to one side, garishly striped like a barber's pole. Next to it is a two-lane bowling green. As I watch, a group of four merry ghosts approach the park, and when one of them leads his girlfriend up the steps to the guillotine, I can guess what is going to come next.

I enter the alchemy shop, the little bell over the door dinging as I close it behind me. A fat middle-aged man, bald like an egg but with bushy muttonchops, stands behind the counter. He wears a leather apron.

All kinds of odd items line the shelves, from wands to ritual daggers. The shop smells of herbs and incense, a pungent but welcome relief from the street stench. I breathe it in, grateful for the respite.

"Help you?" the shopkeep inquires, a note of suspicion creeping into his voice.

I remember ghosts aren't supposed to breathe, so I force a smile and pull out my list. "Um, yeah. I need everything on this list."

"Not for you then?"

"No, it's... for a friend." I set the list on the counter, being careful not to touch the shopkeep's beefy hand as he reaches for the parchment.

He reads over the list and grunts. "Pricey! You rich or is your 'friend' footing the bill?"

"I've got coin." I pull out the sack and toss it on the counter. "That should be enough drachmas to cover it."

The shopkeep opens the bag, spilling out the coins. He counts them into neat little stacks of ten, taking his time, lining them up just right. I get bored and make the mistake of looking out the window.

Across the street.

Into the park.

There's a meaty *thwack* as the guillotine chops off one of the ghost-women's heads. I avert my eyes and take an involuntary step back, bumping into a shelf.

The shopkeep looks up in annoyance.

"Sorry," I mutter.

"That nonsense bother you?" He seems to have finished counting the coins, and proceeds to make them all disappear but one.

"No," I lie. "Not really. I mean…"

"Yeah?"

"I thought violence wasn't allowed on Mercy Street."

"It's not."

"What do you call that?" I say, jerking my thumb over my shoulder toward the park.

"That?" the shopkeep chuckles. "That's consensual. The law only applies to harming citizens against their will."

"Oh, right. I, uh, must have forgotten."

"Say, you really are new here, aren't you?"

"You can tell?"

He snorts and pushes the last remaining coin toward me, the sound of metal scraping loud against the wooden counter. He doesn't let go of the coin but keeps two fingers on it as if daring me to take it.

"What's that?"

"Your change. Don't spend it all in one place—unless it's here." He chuckles at his own joke. When I don't reach for the coin, he shrugs and takes his fingers away. "Going to be a minute to fill your order. Try not to knock anything over, because your change won't cover the damages."

I take the coin. "I'll be careful."

He looks me up and down, shakes his head, then walks through a curtain into the stockroom. From across the street, I hear another *thwack* as another head comes free of its neck. I shudder, then peruse the shelves to pass the time. I'm holding up a prehistoric spider trapped in amber when something else catches my interest.

Crystals.

Long, sharp, and deadly.

There are three of them, all deep crimson, pointed like spikes. There's something special about them. Something I can sense, but can't name. I look over my shoulder, hear the shopkeep in the stock room, and and decide to steal the crystals as replacements for the ones I lost fighting Gyges and the harpies on the Cliffs of Pain.

My earth magic allows me to conceal the crystals between my knuckles, sliding between the bones, merging with my flesh. These crystals feel different than the ones I've used before. Stronger. More powerful. *More magic.* I'm just sliding the last one in when I hear the shopkeep pass through the curtain. I finish hiding it, then turn around with what I hope isn't a guilty expression. "That was fast. Got everything?"

The shopkeep grunts as he sets a wooden box filled with supplies on the counter. "I'm guessing this isn't your friend's first experiment?"

"Well, no... but we're just kind of messing around."

The shopkeep gives me a puzzled look. "Messing around? Are you serious? Do you know what this stuff does?"

"No, but I have a feeling I'm going to find out." I pick up the box and leave the shop, the bell over the door jangling behind me.

"Hey!" a voice says from below eye level.

I look down and don't see anyone. Then I peer around the box and see a severed head. It's one of the ghost-women from the park.

"Hey," she says again. "Do me a favor and toss me back."

I look across the street and see her male companions waving at me. "Over here!" one calls, and the other says, "You can kick her if you don't want to set down the box." The second man carries his girlfriend's dripping head by her long blonde hair.

I stare down at the head at my feet. The ghost smiles up through bloodstained teeth. "Go on," she urges. "Kick me, handsome! I won't mind."

I back away, then turn to run. When I get to the end of the block and look back, I see the men rolling their girlfriend's heads toward the bowling pins.

I hate this town. I hate it so much.

I'm so lost in thought, so torn between worrying about Mark and the future—not to mention what I've just seen—that I don't watch where I'm going.

I walk right through a ghost, but this one's a miserable-looking cripple pushing herself along the street on a hand cart. Her greasy dark hair hangs like a curtain over her face. The girl's legs are missing, two savagely scarred stumps sticking out of her filthy dress.

"Spare change?" she moans, seemingly oblivious to the fact I walked right through her.

I reach into my pocket and toss my last coin to the beggar girl. She bends over and picks up the coin, mumbling words of gratitude. I'm walking away when the girl says something else.

My name.

I stop, not sure I heard her right. When I turn around, I know I did. The beggar has brushed the tangled mop of hair back to reveal a once-pretty face.

A face I know.

Brenda Larson. The girl from gym class at Axios. The one Mr. Cross partnered with my rival, Blake Masters, in the wall-climbing competition. Only Inquisitor Anton had rigged the wall, trapped it, and Blake and Brenda had died that day. A buzzsaw sheared off her legs at the knee, then an avalanche had sent her and Blake tumbling to the gym floor nearly fifty feet below. I can still hear the distant crunch, the pop of two red balloons wetly bursting as the crowd goes wild. It was a lifetime ago.

"Andrus?" Brenda says my name again, pushing her ruined body through the dirty street. "Is that you?"

I don't know what to say, so I don't say anything. I just stand there, staring. Wanting to run. Wanting to help. Brenda doesn't deserve this fate, doesn't deserve to be in Murder Town. She never killed anyone, never wanted to. Then I remember the town isn't just for killers, it's for victims. Victims who want to suffer, who feel they deserve to, and my heart goes out to Brenda.

"It's me," I say as my old classmate rolls up.

"You're dead too," she says, then giggles a bit madly before biting down on her gruesome humor. "What happened? Did the wall get you too?"

"No."

Brenda acts like she didn't hear me or it isn't important. "They cheated! The wall... it was rigged. I... I almost made it."

"You almost did."

"Everything's a blur after I lost my legs. I was just dead weight. In shock. Blake blames me, you know. For that, for falling, for everything."

"Blake never did like losing."

"It was my fault... I wasn't good enough. Didn't train hard enough. Even though the school cheated."

"I'm sorry, Brenda. You don't deserve this."

She wipes away tears. "Yes, I do, but it's kind of you to say. Blake... he used to say nice things to me, before... before we fell. He made me believe we could do it. We could win."

"Is he here?" I look around wildly, worried I'll see Blake, that he'll be wanting revenge, but all I see are strangers who pay us no mind.

"Blake's around. He's always around." She giggles again, sounding less and less sane. "Andrus?"

"Yeah?"

"I wish it had been you."

At first, I think Brenda means she wishes it was me who had been cut in half and crushed by rocks, but the way she's looking at me, I know that's not it.

"I wish you'd been my partner," she says, confirming it. "Not Blake. Then I'd be alive. We'd both be, and I wouldn't be here, like this... I don't know anyone here except Blake. He takes care of me, and I take care of him. Forever. That's kind of like love, isn't it?"

I don't reply.

Brenda slumps her shoulders in despair. "Maybe... I don't know."

"What?"

"Maybe since you're here now, maybe we can be together. You know, instead of me and Blake." The look she gives me is so desperate, so beyond despair, I want to reach out to her but know I can't.

"I'm not mad, you know. I'm not mad at you, or even Blake. I'm mad at myself. I had everything, and thought I'd have it forever. Now I have this... But you, Andrus! You and me, we could have something together. *Something special.* I... I know I was stuck-up to you before. I was a real bitch, but I'm not so bad. Not really. Death has a way of humbling us."

Before I can react, Brenda's arms snake out to wrap around my leg. Only they pass right through me.

Brenda stares at her arms, still wavering from interacting with solid flesh, then up at me. "You!" she gasps. "You're not dead! But how? How, Andrus? How can you be here, alive?"

I back away from her.

She pushes herself after me, red-rimmed eyes wide with the madness of hope. "Did you come to save me? Is that it? Is that why you've come?" And before I can answer, she adds, "Can you bring me back to life? I know where my legs are. We can go get them. They're not far. I don't want to be here anymore."

I shake my head. "I can't, Brenda. I'm sorry."

Her eyes narrow. "You don't mean that! You're just scared. Don't be. Not of me. I told you, I don't blame you for letting me die. I know you had to. It was either me or you, you or me... but that was then. This is now. Don't you see? Everything is different."

"If you don't want to be here," I tell her, "you don't have to be. There's a whole other world beyond these walls, a whole other afterlife just waiting for you..."

Her expression hardens. "Liar! Give me my life back. *I died for you.* Take me with you or I'll scream. I mean it."

She does. I can still hear Brenda shrieking a block later as I run for my life—and Mark's.

10

IGNORE THE SCREAMS

I RUN THE FIRST FEW BLOCKS, but when I don't see any pursuit, I walk the rest of the way. Trying not to draw attention. Trying not to look back over my shoulder. That's the one good thing about Murder Town: People ignore the screams. They blend in like background noise, like the rushing of the river.

As easy as it is for my body to leave Brenda in the past, it's not so simple for my mind. It's not that I haven't thought about her before, or Blake, or that damned wall, it's just that everything's been happening so fast, there hasn't been time to process it all. Still, I can't help but feel guilty.

What she said and the way she said it, hurts. It hurts because I know there's some truth to it. In a way, I did get her killed. Blake too. Not directly, but I set it all in motion... a chain of events that seemed so innocent at first.

A daydream. One little escape from reality. It should have been harmless. They'd never hurt anyone before. Now people are dead. But is it my fault? Or is it just what I am?

A Titan. The son of Cronus and Gaia, born from a rock. It all sounds so completely mad when you think it, and even worse when you say it. But there's no escaping it, no ignoring it, and if I don't keep my mind focused on the big picture, on the quest to save Mark and take down my father's tyranny, I'll go insane. That's why I push Brenda out of my mind—not because I want to, because I have to.

If she really didn't want to be here, she wouldn't—everything I know about the afterlife tells me that. Brenda wants to punish herself more than she wants to be free. And so her ghost pays the price. *Her soul pays the price.* I can't save her, no matter how much I want to. Brenda must save herself.

I hope she does.

As I near Scalpel Close, the hairs on the back of my neck rise. I instinctively turn my head just as Blake Masters rounds the bend. My gym class rival is hurrying along, sword in hand. The look on his face is intense and one I remember well: anger and arrogance. Blake is a bully on a mission, but I can't let him interfere with mine.

Before he can see me, I duck into the dead end. As I run, the alchemical supplies rattle in the box. My eyes strain to pierce the gloom, my feet flying over puddles of blood and loose stacks of bone. Rats look up from the feast, red eyes wide with alarm. They scatter in my wake.

Just ahead, a gore-stained ghost bandaged from head to toe materializes out of the alley wall, moaning to itself, and now I understand what Herophilos meant about the walls having more than ears. *The walls have ghosts.* This one seems more preoccupied with his condition than with me, so I dodge around him and am gone so fast I might as well be a ghost myself.

I don't stop until I get to the unmarked door, the one with the magical lock. Herophilos' door. It won't open, so I bang on it and wait. Knowing Blake is getting closer. He might even be in the alley now. Searching. *For me. For revenge.*

It's not so much Blake as what he represents. My past, my sins. And then there's what my old rival can do... Bring the whole city down on us. Not now. Not when we're so close to bringing Mark back to life. Then at least one of my sins will be erased. Then, maybe I'll have some peace. If only till the next sin, the next disaster.

A key moves in the lock.

I push my way through before the door is even open. "Lock it!" I tell Herophilos. "Now!"

I set the box down on the reception desk, then lean against it, breathing hard. Sweat drips down my forehead.

From the door, the doctor asks, "Problem?"

"Ran into some people I knew. Don't worry, pretty sure I gave them the slip."

"You *think* or you know, Andrus? Were you followed or not?"

"I was, but I told you—I lost them. I made it into the alley just in time."

"What we're about to do is not only very sensitive—it can't be interrupted—but it's also highly illegal to bring the dead back to life."

"But Hades said—"

"What Hades said won't matter until he is here to tell the mob we have been granted an exception, and he can't risk appearing in public until you have struck a decisive blow against Cronus."

"Oh."

"Oh, indeed! At least tell me you didn't use your sword again. That isn't just any blade, you know. It's very distinctive. There are enough residents old enough to recognize the golden sword of Ares when they see it."

"I didn't use it." I don't see the harm in the lie, because as far as I know, no one saw me use it. The alley was empty... wasn't it?

Herophilos moves past me toward the examination room. "Your friend is prepared. Bring the box, and don't say anything to upset him. I need him focused on the task at hand."

Mark smiles when we walk into the room. "Everything go OK? You got all the stuff?"

"All good, buddy." I set down the box on the counter next to the weird specimen jars. "And check this out... I got new claws!" I will the crimson crystals to spring from between the knuckles of my right hand. I hold them up so they gleam in the lamplight. "Pretty cool, huh?"

"Yeah, those are badass! What kind of crystals are those?"

"I'm not sure."

"I thought you were an expert on rocks and crystals?"

"I am, but I've never seen this type before. I found them in the alchemist's shop and..." I notice Herophilos glaring at me and decide not to mention I shoplifted them. "Anyway, I feel better having them."

"I feel better you having them too. That secret weapon has saved us more than once. A sword is good—and a magic one is better—but nothing beats shooting the enemy from a distance."

I retract the crystals, feeling them painlessly merge with my arm. "We'll kick some butt later, when you're back among the living. You just do what the doctor says now, and everything gonna be all right."

"I know. I can't wait."

Herophilos removes supplies from the box. "You'll need to wait outside," the doctor tells me, "until the operation is complete."

"All right." I turn to go, then pause in the doorway. "I'd hug you, man, but... the ghost-thing makes it hard. I just wanted to say you're tough—tougher than you give yourself credit for. You got this."

"Thanks," Mark says. "I've got a good feeling about this. I mean, what's the worst that can happen? It's not like I can die if I'm already dead." He flashes a goofy smile, a smile full of hope, and I can't help but return it.

Herophilos follows me out, closing the exam room door behind us. "Andrus," he says, "I didn't want to say anything in front of the patient, but this operation isn't easy. It's unnatural. And it's going to hurt like hell."

"So what are you saying?"

"I'm saying, no matter what you hear, no matter how you feel, you are not to open that door. Wait for me to come out. It won't be fast, but it will be soon."

"Soon? What's the deal with ghosts and math, anyway? Just give me a time frame I can understand. Minutes, hours, what?"

"Soon," Herophilos repeats. "Sooner than you think, but longer than you wish."

"That's not helpful. You were alive once! You ought to remember how Earth-time works."

The doctor shakes his head. "I do, but time flows differently in Tartarus. Any number I give would be meaningless."

"Yeah, but it will make me feel better."

"Fine. The operation will take five hours, five minutes, and fifty-five seconds. Does that help?"

"I don't know. That seems a little *too* precise. I was hoping for a nice round number."

"Soon is round," Herophilos replies. "Things take however long they take, Andrus. No more, no less. When you're dead, you'll understand that."

"But I'm not dead!"

"*Not yet.*" Herophilos stalks back inside the exam room. To his credit, he doesn't slam the door.

I go to reception and take a seat. There are no magazines, no ancient scrolls, nothing to read or do. So I stare at the alley door, and when nothing bad happens, I stare down the hall toward the exam room. Then I stare at my feet, my hands, the walls, the ceiling.

After a while, I hear Mark scream.

11

PROPHECY

I'M OUT OF MY CHAIR and halfway down the hall before I stop myself. Herophilos said not to interrupt. That it was going to hurt. And Mark had told me how bad it was being inside his dead body. Which is exactly where he is now, only this time, Mark's not in control. He's trapped. Bound to cold flesh, to a past life and future dream.

Is Ares in there now too? Have they summoned him? Is the God of War in as much pain as Mark?

I return to reception. "This really is the waiting room," I mutter. "Soon, my ass!"

I pace, doing my best to ignore my friend's screams. Eventually, the sound drains away, reduced to a low gurgle, like water going down a drain. Then it is gone, and silence hits me. The silence is worse than the screams, because I can't tell what's going on. I have to believe it's a good sign even though it could just as easily mean they failed.

"It will all be worth it," I tell the empty room. "In the end, all the blood and pain and suffering will mean something."

"It will," a sepulchral voice says from the shadows. "It always does."

I jump at the words. The shadows in the corner of the room

deepen, knitting together like a burial shroud, giving birth to the robed form of Hades, God of Death. He fills the room with his presence, with the long cold of the grave.

"Is everything all right? Is Hannah OK? Are the wards down?"

"So many questions," Hades says. "The living are full of them... now the dead are too."

"The dead? What are you talking about?"

His sunken eyes blaze like coals. "The dead of Murder Town know there is someone living here, and that this someone is you, Andrus. You are careless—reckless, like your father!"

"I'm also doing what you said. I'm getting the job done."

"I told you to be *smart*. I told you to be *careful*. That is how we *win*. That is how I *rule*." His breath mists, frosting the air behind his words.

"Ares is back," I tell him. "We prayed him to life. Mark's going to be his priest."

We're interrupted by a blast of shadow, mystic black that runs like ink on water, then takes the form of a raven. Hannah's familiar, Shadow, has returned. The bird lands on the Death God's outstretched arm. He brings it to his ear and the raven speaks in a frantic series of croaks and caws.

"What is it? What's Shadow saying?"

Hades waits for the familiar to finish, then rests his baleful gaze on me. "Gyges is coming."

"I beat him before." I say it with a confidence I don't feel, but the words stamp down the panic rising in me.

"You faced him alone. He has an army with him."

"I have Ares with me."

Hades looks down the hallway to the exam room. "Not yet, you don't. The ritual is complete, but there is an adjustment period. Your friend—and Ares—need time to recover for the bond to stick."

"How much time do we have?"

"Not enough."

"OK. So teleport Mark and me out. You and Hannah have finished taking down the wards, right?"

"Most of them, yes, but not all. That means I still require you to be that distraction we talked about. You have the means to summon Charon?"

I check my pocket for the diamond, then nod.

"Then I suggest you do so as soon as your friend is able to move. I will have the last of the outer wards down by then. Charon will bring you to me, and I will see you from my kingdom and back to Earth safely."

"What about Hannah?"

Hades glowers at me. "My daughter is not your servant, Andrus. She is mine! You do not dictate the terms by which she accompanies you."

"I—I know. I'm just saying, we work well together, and we can use her help. Besides, having Hannah with us gives you eyes and ears on the ground."

"I am a God! I have eyes and ears everywhere."

"Fine, hands and feet then. Someone who loves you and will make sure your plan is carried out."

"You have feelings for her." It's not a question.

I feel myself blush, and briefly consider denying it, then realize it would be pointless. "Yes," I say.

"You love her." Again, it is not a question.

Again, I tell the truth. "Yes, I think so."

"Love is as dangerous as uncertainty," Hades replies. "Both interfere with logic, with truth, with reason. It is not enough to *think* you love her, but to know."

"I do. I do love Hannah."

"Then you must not tell her."

"But why not?"

"Because I need her mind sharp and free from the pain of loss such knowledge would bring."

"What do you mean? Why would telling Hannah hurt her?"

"Because you are going to die, Andrus."

At first, I don't think I heard the Death God right. I feel my face twist into some kind of quizzical half-smile, half-frown. "I don't understand. How can you know that?"

"Because there is a prophecy that says so."

"A prophecy? What prophecy?"

"One I discovered among the treasures I plundered from Cronus after he was defeated millennia ago. It says in order to defeat him, you must sacrifice yourself. You must die for your father to fall."

"I'd like to see that prophecy."

Hades waves his hands and in a burst of shadow, an ancient scroll appears in mine. "You read ancient Greek?" he asks.

"A little..." I open the scroll and my brain swims just looking at it. "Oh, not anything this old. But Mark can."

"Then have him read it to you when he wakes. Remember what I told you, and be ready to sacrifice when the time comes, Andrus. The world is counting on you."

Hades melds into the shadows, leaving me with more questions than answers.

12

GHOSTS DON'T SLEEP

I slump into my chair. Shadow flaps around the room then lands next to me. I pet the raven absently, staring down at the scroll clutched in my other hand. It isn't fair! Everything was crazy, but things were getting better. I thought—I dared to hope—that there might be a happy ending for me.

Not according to the prophecy.

Not according to the moldy old ravings of... who wrote the prophecy? I forgot to ask. I also forgot exactly how I'm supposed to sacrifice myself to defeat Cronus. I get up and pace, startling the bird, who squawks in alarm at the sudden motion.

"Sorry," I mumble, then snort when I see the raven is pacing too. It stops when I stop, tilts its black feathered head and gives me as sympathetic a look as his glowing red eyes can muster. "Look at us," I tell him. "Aren't we a pair? A couple of worry warts."

Shadow flaps his wings and caws in agreement.

The exam room opens and Dr. Herophilos steps out into the hall.

"How's Mark?" I ask.

"Resting." Nothing in the doctor's expression gives any clue as to how the operation went. He crosses to the nurse's desk and pulls a bottle of ouzo and two shot glasses out of the drawer.

"But he's all right?" I ask. "The operation was a success?"

"It was." Herophilos pours us each a shot of the strong Greek liquor. "I am the best surgeon in the Underworld, after all. There was never any doubt in my mind I could do it."

"I'm sorry I doubted you. I was just so worried. And I know you're a good surgeon. You saved Mark's life before, only…"

Herophilos knocks back his shot then glowers a me.

"I, uh, meant you're the best. Not just good."

He raises an eyebrow. "But?"

"Well, um, you know…"

"I believe I do. You are suggesting that brain surgery is one thing, but soul surgery is another?"

I nod. "Something like that."

Herophilos hands me my shot and pours himself another. "*Yamas!*" he toasts, clinking his glass to mine in the traditional Greek toast. "To our health."

"*Yamas.*" I raise the glass to my lips, then remember Hannah's warning about how the living must never eat or drink spirit food. Anyone who does, dies, and may not return to the world of the living.

"It's not spirit drink," Herophilos explains. "I brought this bottle back from my last trip to Earth. See? It runs right through me."

There's a clear puddle on the floor.

"Then why do you drink it?"

"Ouzo—*real ouzo*— is one of the few earthly pleasures I miss. Nothing burns like the real thing. Nothing else has that fresh fragrance of licorice. It reminds me of summer days on the Aegean, the sound of the gulls in my ears, the sparkling blue water, the surf rolling in like a hundred dreams…"

"You should have been a poet." I take the shot, relishing the comforting taste of home. It's definitely real. Definitely the good stuff. It tastes like my father's brand… my foster human father: *George Eaves*. We'd had our differences. We'd loved each other in ways the other couldn't understand, but now that he's gone—him and my foster mother, Carol, both prisoners of the Inquisition—I miss them. I miss them so much! I miss the mansion, the security, the stability of being safe, of having my whole life planned out with no room for adventure or saving the planet.

Dr. Herophilos takes a seat on the other side of the room. He seems weary, and I notice the blue fabric of his tunic is stippled in blood. "You're not wrong," he says with a sigh.

I pour myself another drink. "About what?"

"The surgery. Brain surgery and soul surgery are related fields, but quite different in the end. It took all my skill to pull this procedure off. My work, as usual, is flawless."

"And the rest?"

Herophilos shrugs. "The rest is up to Mark. The patients are always the 'x' factor, Andrus. Some live, some die, some hover between before making up their minds which way to go. But your friend is strong. I have every confidence he'll pull through. I'd stake my reputation on it."

I sit in a chair opposite Herophilos, feeling every bit as drained and every bit as relieved as I did after my battle on the Bridge of Burnt Souls. Mark's going to make it. He has to.

"Hades was here," Herophilos says.

I drain my glass at the mention of his name. "How did you know?"

"Because only the God of Death and his servants can get past my wards. I knew the instant they were breached, but was too busy to come out and greet him. I assumed you two needed time to confer."

"Confer?"

Herophilos spreads his hands in a sweeping gesture. The long, delicate fingers are stained with Mark's blood. "On the plan. Whatever grand scheme he is about to embark on."

I look at the bottle of ouzo longingly, but know better than to get drunk now, no matter how much I might feel like it. "How well do you know Hades?"

"As well as any man can know Death."

"And you trust him?"

"Hades is a schemer, Andrus. He's hard and he's cold, but he's the best ruler Tartarus ever had. He loves the dead and cares for us as if we were his children—which we are, in a way. More than that, *he listens*, and how many Gods can say that?"

"Not many," I agree.

"Precisely! You can talk to him, reason with him, all without fear of being unreasonably tortured and devoured. Try doing that with Cronus... Anyway, you did the right thing freeing Hades. The Kingdom of the Dead owes you. *I owe you.*"

We sit in silence while a question forms in my mind. When it's ready, I ask, "You said Hades is the best ruler Tartarus ever had, but what about Earth? Hades may be great at managing the dead, but what about the living?"

Herophilos shrugs. "He never had the chance. His brothers—Zeus and Poseidon—cheated him. Vain, lusty, hot-tempered brutes! It's always the extroverts who ruin everything. They're the reason the world is as violent as it is, and as chaotic, like the storms and waves they sprang from. They had a chance, Andrus! A chance to fix the mistakes of the past, the past the Titans made. Instead, they put a bandage on it, but the wound... *the wound festered*. It was only a matter of time until man turned away from the Gods and the Titans burst free."

I sigh. "That's what Hades said, only without the medical analogy."

Herophilos smirks. "Forgive me, my bedside manner is a little rusty. Why don't you tell me what's really ailing you?"

"It's that obvious?"

"I'm no psychiatrist, but I'm willing to listen."

I get up and hand him the scroll.

The doctor unfurls it, the smirk fading, replaced by a frown. He hands it back to me.

"Well?" I ask, hoping for a translation, but what I get instead is a diagnosis.

"You're afraid to die."

I nod, forgetting about the translation as emotion washes over me. "It's not fair! I feel like I was finally starting to live, now this..."

"We're all afraid to die," Herophilos says, "until we do."

"And then?"

"Then *this*, or whatever afterlife you feel you've earned. It's a relief, really. Every day living is another day dying—getting older, slower, watching everything and everyone you love crumble to dust. But when you're dead, you're dead. Everything and everyone is back again, free again, with limitless possibilities…"

I let that sink in. "Can I ask you something, doc?"

"It's *doctor*," he corrects me, "but yes, you may."

"Why do you stay here, in Murder Town?"

He leans back in his chair and looks up at the ceiling. "That, my friend, is a tale long in the telling. Oh, I know I could 'move on' to some other simple, more serene place, but what would I do there? What would I be?"

"What about your family? Your friends? Don't you miss them?"

He shakes his head. "I had none, not in life. I had my work. It was enough then, it is enough now. I was never a social creature, Andrus. Hades and I are a lot alike in that way. We prefer to live in our heads, only coming out every once in a while to share some new discovery, some fresh stroke of genius."

"I see."

"Actually, I'm not sure you do. I don't think anyone who isn't like me can understand. What we do—*what I do*—some people call monstrous, because they don't understand. They see the horror of now instead of the hope for the future." He gets up to pour himself another shot. "I'm not the mad butcher some paint me to be. Everything I did, everything I do, I do for a reason…"

I hold out my glass for a refill. The doctor pours, then sits on the desk. We nurse our drinks.

After a while, the doctor says, "People can hate me and fear me and tarnish my name, but when they need my help, do I turn them away? Of course not! What I do is for them—all of them. The whole stinking, miserable, ungrateful lot!" Herophilos smiles when he says this, and as cantankerous as it sounds, there's no venom in the words, and I begin to see he's not angry at the world. He's mystified.

Genuinely mystified people can't see the value in his work, or his sacrifice.

And that makes me wonder... *will the world see the value in mine?*

Almost as an afterthought, I mention the impending arrival of Gyges and his army. Herophilos nods, saying it was only a matter of time, but isn't everything?

I can't argue with that. I send Shadow out to keep an eye on things then ask, "How quickly will Mark be awake and ready to move?"

I can tell Herophilos starts to say, "Soon," then stops himself. "In Earth time? A few hours. As his physician, I wouldn't advise anything faster."

"All right." I begin to pace, plotting our next move, our great escape from the city.

Herophilos watches me. "May I make a suggestion?"

"Sure."

"No doubt the great philosophers disagree, but I do believe it is possible to overthink things. The grave comes soon enough. No point worrying yourself into one early."

I stop pacing. "What do you recommend?"

The doctor shrugs. "Sleep."

"Sleep? Seriously, at a time like this, you're telling me to sleep?"

"I'm not telling you to do anything. I'm suggesting. Think about it: You know danger is coming. You also know what that danger is and approximately when it will arrive. You also know that due to Mark's condition, you can't really do anything about it."

"So?"

"You have a few hours. Would you rather spend it worrying or making sure you're rested enough to face the danger when it comes?"

He has a point.

"Normally," he goes on, "I'd prescribe a sedative, but we can't have you groggy when it's time to run."

I look at the bottle of ouzo.

"I wouldn't advise any more of that either."

"You have a bedroom?"

"Ghosts don't sleep, Andrus."

"What do you do?"

"We rest when we wish or when we are forced… It is a dormant state, akin to sleep, and with similar restorative effects. Indeed, there are many ghosts who still refer to it as 'sleep' and go to bed as they did in life, but the longer you are dead, the less need you have for old habits, old rituals…" He notices my impatience, and gestures to the floor. "Unfortunately, I only have this, but you're welcome to it."

"I want to see Mark first."

"By all means," Herophilos says, gesturing toward the hall. "Put your mind at ease."

I walk down the hall, mind racing with thoughts, with worries, but I put them out of my head when I see Mark resting comfortably on the examination table. His body is inked in mystic symbols and there is a livid white scar over his heart where I plunged the sword in. And he's breathing! His chest rises and falls at regular intervals. It sounds normal, not labored at all.

"We did it," I whisper. "You made it, buddy!"

Mark doesn't answer, but he doesn't need to. Just seeing him alive is enough to untangle the knot of emotion caught up inside me. Maybe it's that, or maybe it's the ouzo, but I can't stand anymore. At first I sit, leaning against the cabinet, watching him sleep, then I've got my backpack off, then I'm using it as a pillow, then I'm falling inside myself… down to somewhere else.

13

THE TRUE EVIL

I LAND ON TOP OF A FROZEN LAKE hard enough to crack the ice, but not my bones. Above me is a gloomy palace built on volcanic rock that rises from the center of the lake. It's Hades' castle, or at least it was. Now it belongs to Cronus. And this is Lake Cocytus, where the Gods imprisoned the Titans millennia ago...

"Andrus..."

I hear my father call my name, hear it echo across the lake, across space and time. I put my hands over my ears to block the sound, but that's no good. Cronus' voice is in my head.

"Andrus..."

"Get out of my head!" I shout, but when I shut my eyes, I see his: three blinding, blazing orbs that burn like the sun. His unblinking gaze holds me, binds me like a curse. I can't move. Can't open my eyes, but I can hear the ice breaking all around me. Worse, I can feel it...

"Hades is using you," Cronus warns. "Once your usefulness is at an end, he will bury you here, as he buried me and all our kind. In the ice. In the darkness."

"You're lying!"

Cronus laughs, and it is the sound of thunder. "You are my son.

Join me, join all your brothers and sisters. See the truth. Experience what it means to be a Titan!"

"No!"

"The Olympians will never accept you. There is no future with them. Your future—*your destiny*—lies with me. As my son, my emissary, my Bridge Between Worlds!"

"I won't help you conquer new worlds! I'll never serve you."

"Everyone serves me, Andrus. One way or another. In life, in death, and beyond. Even the Gods serve me."

"How?"

"The dead Gods serve as an example to my enemies. The live ones—what few remain—serve to teach you your true place."

"They are my allies." For some reason, I don't say "friends," even though that's what I want them to be.

Again, Cronus laughs, his voice rising like the wind. "You are their pawn! They need one of my bloodline to break my wards and distract my armies. Oh, I know of Hades' plan! I have foreseen it, just as I have foreseen his prophecy…"

"What do you know about that?"

Cronus' three eyes blaze, and now, in the darkness of my mind, the King of the Titans looms over me in all his monstrous, black-scaled glory. "I know it says you must die to defeat me. But would you? Would you really die for me? For them? Because once you sacrifice yourself, you'll be dead. Who wins then?"

"Humanity."

"No, my son. Once you are dead, and I am dead, and all your brothers and sisters, who will be left to rule? *Hades.* He is not interested in sharing power. That is why he will not bring back Zeus and Poseidon, or the rest of the Gods save Ares, and only because he needs him… for the moment. Once the Titans are gone, Ares will join us in death, as will all humanity."

"What?"

"Hades did not tell you? No, of course he didn't. If you were really his ally, perhaps he would have. But only a fool tells a pawn his true plan…"

Cronus smiles his shark smile, waiting for me to ask the question he knows I must ask.

"What is Hades' true plan?"

"To kill, and kill, and kill. He is the God of Death, and the dead must obey his commands. What better way to ensure loyal subjects than to kill every last man, woman, and child? Then, they cannot worship other Gods. Then, all threats to his rule vanish like smoke on the wind! And with each death, Hades' power grows. Your death paves the way for the deaths of every living creature. So tell me, who is the true evil?" His point made, Cronus releases me from his psychic grip.

I open my eyes. I'm still on the frozen lake. Alone, but in terrible danger. The ice cracks, spiderwebbing out in a dozen directions, a hundred zig-zag lines. I have to get up. I have to get back to Mark, to Murder Town.

To Earth.

I scrabble on hands and knees, feeling the chill, the primal numbing cold of the Cocytus, and I begin to understand how it could trap even Titans in its frozen depths.

I get to my feet, staggering forward. Slipping, sliding. Crunching on snow, cracking through ice. I yank my foot back and stumble on. Only now there are shadows rising up from the depths, shadows that become shapes, shapes that become bodies. The bodies of a million dead bob below my feet, just under the ice.

The entire human race.

All here.

All dead.

I see my adopted parents. I see Mark, Lucy, and yes, even Hannah. So blue, so cold, so lonely in her frozen tomb. But the worst face I recognize is my own. *I'm under the ice with them.* Trapped. Dead forever. The terror is too much. And as I scream, the sound of my fear shatters the ice. It shatters it and sends me plunging down...

Down, into the dark.

Into the deep.

Into the end.

PART II

SACRIFICE

14

DOCTOR'S ORDERS

I wake with a start, a frozen scream caught in my throat. Only it's not just a scream, it's water. *Ice water from the lake.* I'm drenched from head to toe. I roll on my side, coughing and sputtering. Shivering from the cold. But how is this possible? I've always gone places in my dreams before... far places, distant and magical. But only in my head, never with my body.

Did I somehow travel to Lake Cocytus, or did I bring part of the lake to me? I'm in the examination room. Mark is still resting, still out of it, and I'm feeling pretty out of it myself...

I am the Bridge Between Worlds. I'm supposed to have the power to travel to other places, other dimensions, but I've never been able to do it before. I've carved out tunnels, sure, but through earth and stone, not time and space. What if I've somehow unlocked that ability? What if I can use it to get Mark and me out of Murder Town and back to Earth without relying on Charon and Hades?

I reach inside myself for the power, but find only numb, empty space. Maybe I used it up. Maybe it needs time... time to recharge. What if when I can access it, I can't control it? I can't worry about that now. We'll stick with the original plan. Hades' plan.

Except... *What if Cronus is right?*

Before I can take the thought any further, Mark sits up and opens his eyes. They glow red-gold, the eyes of Ares, God of War. He lets out a strangled gasp, face contorting in pain before the translucent ghost-mask Hannah gave him reforms over his face. The mask is amorphous and invisible except when first activated. It converts the toxic gasses of Tartarus into breathable air, with the added benefit of making Mark look like a ghost.

I hadn't thought about the mask since Hannah had first given it to him in the cave under Bronson Canyon, but now I'm glad to see it's still in place. The mask doesn't work on the dead, so the fact it had to reboot itself means Mark is alive. The monsters might kill him, but at least the atmosphere can't.

Shadow flaps into the room, cawing frantically. Dr. Herophilos follows the raven, a grave look on his face. I look from one to the next, and know the monsters are here. It's time to go.

"I packed you a bag," Herophilos says. "It's by the door. Some medical supplies you might need, some potions Mark definitely will."

Mark turns his head toward the doctor, the red-gold fading until they return to their normal color. "Ugh… what? Potions?"

"One a day," Herophilos explains. "Take your first dose before you leave the office."

"What's it do?" I ask.

"It will help Mark's body heal and cement the spiritual bonding process… the possession. It's designed to speed the physical and psychic recovery process."

"Thank you," Mark says, "for everything."

"Me too. Thanks, doctor."

He smiles. "My pleasure… Andrus, what happened to you? What are you covered in? Is that water?"

"Long story," I say. "We don't have time to get into it now. Thanks again."

Mark is slow getting dressed but waves me off when I try to help him. "I can do it," he insists. "Just… give me a minute. Everything's still a little woozy."

"You all right?"

He nods.

"Run your symptoms by Herophilos while I grab a dose of that potion."

Shadow squawks and shoots ahead of me. He lands on a chair by the reception room door and begins strutting anxiously.

"I know," I tell him. "We're hurrying!"

The black bird squawks again. I ignore him and head for the backpack by the door. It's full of ointments and bandages, needle and thread for stitching wounds, the usual emergency field kit. There's also a map of Murder Town with the best routes out of the city clearly marked. But I came for the potions. I find them in a padded case containing eight glass vials. Four on top, four below, with a thick layer of cloth in-between. I grab one and head to the exam room.

"Everything OK?" I ask the doctor.

Herophilos says nausea and lightheadedness are normal, as is the burning sensation around his chest wound. "Nothing to be concerned about," he adds, "though Mark should avoid strenuous activity for the next several days."

"Not gonna happen, but I'll try to keep him out of as much danger as possible." I hand Mark the potion. It's blue and glows faintly. "Here, drink this."

Mark uncorks the top and sniffs it, makes a face, then downs the entire vial. His expression worsens, but he manages to keep it down. He swallows hard, then coughs. "*Gah!* What the… That's horrible!"

"Doctor's orders," I tell him. "Come on, man. Let's go."

Herophilos follows us to the door since only his magic key can get us past the wards. As he turns the key in the lock, the mystic wards glow, then fade into the wood. "Be careful," he urges. "You have no idea what this town can be like."

I snort. "Oh, I think I do."

15

RATS

SHADOW FLIES OVERHEAD as Mark and I head down the alley. I stop and pull the diamond from my pocket.

"What's up?" Mark asks.

"It might take Charon a while to show up once we toss this in the river."

"Yeah, so?"

"So we might not have a while."

Mark frowns, mulling the idea over, then brightens.

"You see where I'm going with this?"

"Yeah," he says. "If I hadn't just come back from the dead, I would have gotten it sooner. You think we should have Shadow fly ahead and use the diamond. That way, Charon will be ready when we are."

I nod.

Mark whistles to call Shadow back from scouting up ahead. I give Hannah's raven the diamond and Mark tells it what to do. The bird tilts its head and caws something back.

"What's he saying?" I ask.

"Shadow says it's a good idea, but reckless. If he flies to the river, he can't scout ahead."

The familiar bobs his beak up and down.

"We'll just have to take our chances. Tell him to summon Charon, then fly back."

"Where? Are we going to wait for him here?"

"No, tell him to find us." I pull out the map Herophilos gave me and trace the route so Shadow can see which way we're going. "If we aren't here," I point at one of the bridges out of town, "then meet us here." I point at an alternate route to a different bridge. "Or here." I point to a third bridge. "We'll be at or enroute to one of them, OK?"

Mark relays the information to Shadow, and the raven flies off, still clutching the diamond. "I hope that was the right move," he says.

I shrug. "It is or it isn't. We'll find out soon enough. Did you familiarize yourself with the map in case we get separated?"

"Better let me have another look." Mark goes over the routes again, then nods. "Right. Got it."

I fold the map and stuff it in my pocket. We pass the other doctor's offices, the clinics and medical supply houses, and the alley's the same, but there's something different in the air. Something electric, like the whole town is shot through with adrenaline.

When we get to the edge of Scalpel Close, I turn to Mark and whisper, "Just act casual. Don't draw attention, and don't touch anyone. You're not a ghost anymore, so they'll know something's up."

We step onto Mercy Street. I'm annoyed there aren't more ghosts around to give us cover. It's not nearly as crowded as it was the last time. Maybe because the ghosts sense something big is about to happen...

We're headed away from the Market District, back the way we came when we first entered Murder Town. We pass the same hunchback selling rats on a stick. "Live rats!" he calls. "Get your live rats here! The perfect treat for the perfect day... Watch them squirm! Watch them suffer..." He tries to shove one of the poor impaled creatures at me, but I wave him off. "Rats," he warns, "either you get them, or they get you!"

About half a block later, the hunchback is proven right when I see Blake Masters standing at the corner. Good old Blake, the bully and the bastard. He was hard enough to avoid when he was alive, and he's proving just as difficult in death.

Blake is talking to Captain Nessus. The ram-headed centaur is gray-furred, shaggy, and just as horrible as I remember. And he's not alone. Of course not. Nessus is never alone. His savage brothers, Democ and Ruvo, are with him, just as evil if not as smart. And they've got an entire squad of centaurs to back them up. The only good news is none of them have noticed us yet.

I can't make out what Blake is saying, but it's got to be something about me. Ratting me out for a reward, or maybe from sheer spite.

"What do we do?" Mark asks.

I look around for an alley. Murder Town is riddled with them, but now that we need one, there aren't any between us and the centaurs.

"New plan," I hiss. "Back the way we came, then take an alternate route to the river."

We do a casual about-face and head toward Scalpel Close.

"Change your mind?" the hunchback asks as we pass his stall. "All rats fresh! Impaled while you wait..."

I wave him off again, unable to hide my disgust.

"What's the matter? My rats not good enough for you?"

We keep walking while the hunchback hurls curses. Not good. He's going to attract attention. The wrong kind, as if there's any other in this nightmare place.

A flock of harpies wings overhead, the familiar shriek of the vulture-women loud in my ears. But they pass on by.

"It's OK," I tell Mark. "We're OK. Just a little further..."

There's an alley up ahead. I don't know where it leads or if it's a dead end. At the rate things are going, it could be a literal dead end, but we have to chance it. It's not safe to stay on Mercy Street.

Only when we get to the alley, we see that it's occupied. A male ghost dressed in dark Victorian clothes and a fancy top hat is butchering a scantily-clad female ghost with a straight razor.

"Please tell me that's not Jack the Ripper," Mark says.

There's no way to get past the grisly scene without walking

through them, which is as good as yelling to the the centaurs, "Hey! Look over here."

"Never mind," I whisper to Mark. "We'll take the next one."

We don't make it more than thirty feet before we see a pair of cyclopes lumber into view. They may only have one eye each, but that's enough to spot us. The brutish giants break into a run, battle axes raised. "Over here!" the one on the left shouts. "Found them!" the other roars.

For a second, I think we can run around the giants, but a half-dozen more come around the corner, and that's too many. The monsters fill Mercy Street, cutting us off from Scalpel Close and the rest of Murder Town.

We turn and run, only now Nessus and his centaurs are closing in from the opposite direction. Behind them, Blake points at us and gloats.

We turn back toward the cyclopes. "The alley!" I yell. Mark and I make it just before the cyclopes do, and they're too big to enter. Even the centaurs will have to go single file through it. So that creates a traffic jam that buy us time to escape.

We run through the demented mad slasher and his beautiful victim, causing their outlines to shift and shimmer. They stop their savage game and begin to yell and chase after us. "Fresh meat!" they scream. "Live victims!"

Ahead, doors and windows in the alley pop open, revealing ghosts in various states of murder or being murdered. They all look shocked, which for this town, I'm sure is saying a lot. But their shock doesn't last long, just long enough for us to rush past them, down the narrow twisting turns, past reeking puddles and rancid garbage, deeper into the depths of Murder Town. Then they're coming after us, weapons raised, shrieking and laughing the cries of the damned. Old ones, young ones, and every kind in-between, all out for blood.

Our blood.

"The whole city's coming down on us!" Mark says. "This alley better lead somewhere."

But it doesn't. It dead-ends at a door. Next to the door is a dumpster overflowing with severed arms and legs. A sign on the wall reads, DR. CRIPPEN'S CRIPPLINGS. DELIVERIES ONLY. PATIENTS USE ENTRANCE ON SCALPEL CLOSE.

"We'll cut through here," I say. When the door proves to be locked, I pull out my magic sword and chop through the wood. We barge into the doctor's office, passing recovery rooms with groaning patients missing various limbs.

There are multiple hallways and we end up taking one that brings us into an operating room, only it's not just a room, but a theater, with rows of seats for leering ghouls to watch the mad Doctor Crippen at work.

He's a bald, beady-eyed man, pudgy and sweaty, and he's bending over a pretty patient on the operating table. A patient I recognize: Brenda Larson. Somehow, she grew her legs back and is having them removed again, which—to my horror—I realize must be something she does every day to punish herself.

"Andrus!" Brenda sits up on the table—clearly not even anesthetized for the horrific procedure. "Mark! What the—"

My heart goes out to her, and under less urgent circumstances, I might be tempted to stop and help, but I know Brenda's insane, and I know she wants revenge. And nothing I say in the next few seconds can change that.

"Get them, you fools!" she howls. "They're alive!"

The doctor, the grinning ghouls in the gallery, they all spring into action. Even Brenda gets up off the operating table and gives chase.

Mark and I race through the maze of offices until we hit reception. We blow past the startled nurse and out the front door into Scalpel Close.

"Which way?" Mark shouts. "We could hide out with Herophilos..."

Somewhere in the distance, I hear the harpies coming.

"They'd find us eventually," I rasp back. "Come on, back to Mercy Street!"

Only there's no mercy on Mercy Street. A bunch of ghosts are marching down the mouth of the alley, hungry for murder.

We run down Scalpel Close, toward the office of Dr. Herophilos. The ghosts from Dr Crippen's join the frenzied mob behind us. Mark slows, thinking I changed my mind, but I haven't. I can't implicate Herophilos in all this, and besides, barricading ourselves in his office won't buy us much time. His wards might be strong enough to keep out the ghosts and monsters, but how long could they hold against Gyges, Cronus, or the rest of the Titans?

No, hiding won't work.

Not when I have a better idea…

16

FIGHTING CRAZY WITH CRAZY

"Where are you going?" Mark shouts. He slows down when we get to Herophilos' door, but not me. I keep going until I get to the end of the alley, to the magically locked door of the MURDER TOWN ASYLUM FOR THE ETERNALLY INSANE.

Mark catches up to me and starts to ask what I'm doing, then gasps. "Holy shit," he says. "Um, you know this is crazy, right?"

"You've heard of fighting fire with fire, right?"

Mark nods.

"So we're fighting crazy with crazy. This place holds all the worst, most vicious madmen... We let them out, and let them do our fighting for us."

"Won't they try to kill us?"

"No doubt! But first, they gotta catch us." I look up at the stone walls of the alley as phase two of my plan pops into my head.

"How are we gonna do that?" Mark asks. "If we can't go back the way we came, and we can't stay here, then what..."

Mark follows my gaze. Straight up the alley walls. He gulps. "Really?"

"Yup. Just like gym class. You just climb on my back and I'll carry you up."

Mark curses in resignation. "Walls! Why does it always have to be walls?"

"Hey, man! Don't worry about it. You'll just be along for the ride."

We hear the sound of ghosts coming down the alley. Coming to kill us, to make us like them so they can kill us all over again. Forever and ever.

I use my sword, the magic golden sword of Ares, to hack at the door. The wards are stronger than I thought, and resist my blows, though I can see some weaken and others fail as their glow fades. "This is taking too long," I mutter.

"Perhaps I can help." Mark says the words, but it's the deep, grim voice of Ares, and it is his red-gold eyes that lock onto mine. He stretches out his hand and from out of nowhere, my sword's twin materializes in his hand, the golden blade blazing to life.

We both hack at the door, Ares and I, and now the wards are failing faster. We hack through the last of them just as the bloodthirsty ghosts arrive.

I throw open the asylum door, shouting, "You're free! Free to kill, free to destroy! Avenge yourselves! Avenge!"

My words ring out down the long dark hallway, and at first, I think it's not going to work, that maybe the prisoners are all individually locked into their cells, but then I hear the babbling chaos of the crazed, the doomed, those shattered souls who are trapped beyond insanity into eternal madness. Cell doors are thrown open, releasing kill-crazy shadows, stalking fiends that lurch forth in a frenzy of horror.

"Come out!" I yell. "Come out and kill!"

We sheathe our swords, and I sink my hands into the stone wall. "Hop on," I tell Mark, who is no longer Ares but himself again. He stands there, looking confused, but the sound of hate-hungry ghosts snaps him out of it.

He climbs on my back and we begin to climb. Up the asylum wall and out of the alley. Beneath us, I hear the surprised howl of the mob as the prisoners rush them. The street becomes a bloodbath, a deathmatch for dueling ghosts.

A few desperate knives and bottles crash and clatter against the wall near us, but then we're too high, my earth magic making my fingers and boots sink into the stone as if it were clay.

"Yeah," Mark says in my ear. "Remind me never to do this again."

"What? Climbing?"

"Climbing, dying... All of it, man! Just all of it."

A few minutes latter, we make it to the top, to the asylum's roof, and take a moment to recover.

"You all right?" I ask. "You didn't stay Ares long."

He shrugs. "Didn't need to. Gotta conserve his power; we're still recovering. I don't think doing that helped, but it's not like we had a choice. Did I tell you your plan was crazy?"

"Pretty sure you did. Sorry, it was all I could think of on short notice."

"Yeah, well, it worked. That's all that matters." He peers over the side. "Wow, look at 'em go! They're really tearing each other apart."

"You see Blake or Brenda?" I don't bother to look myself. I'm focusing my gaze along the rooftops toward the river. Working on the next plan, the next move.

"Hard to tell," Mark replies. "There's too many of 'em. That sucks Brenda is here. What happened back at Axios wasn't her fault."

"Doesn't matter. She *believes* she belongs here, so that's where she'll stay. Right and wrong have nothing to do with it. It's all about choice." As I say it, I flashback to my dream, to the three-eyed face of my father watching me with his cunning, razor-toothed grin. I shudder at the memory of him, of being buried in ice. "We gotta go."

Mark tears his gaze from the fighting below. "Let me guess: more climbing?"

"Nah... well, not much." I point a path over the rooftops. "If we can jump from roof to roof, we can avoid the ghosts *and* the monsters."

"Not all of them," Marks reminds me.

Right on cue, there's an hideous cackling from above.

17

THEM AGAIN

I WHIRL as the harpies dive toward us. There are three of them and two of us. Mark draws his sword, but I raise my right hand and make a fist. The crimson crystals slide out between my knuckles. I aim for the lead harpy and fire the first crystal. It shears through her black feathered ribs, shredding organs, sending the bird-woman into a shrieking death spiral to the alley below.

I target the next harpy and the next, the remaining crystals striking true. Both of the cruel-beaked monsters sprawl in death at our feet.

Mark stands there, holding his sword, ready for a fight that's already over. He looks around for an enemy, but there aren't any, except the rampaging ghosts in the alley below. "OK..." Marks says, sheathing his blade. "That was easy."

I bend down next to the dead harpies and retrieve the crystals from between their ribs. They slide out easily, but are drenched in oily black monster blood.

Mark grimaces. "You might want to get that gore off before you go sticking them back under your skin... Just saying."

I do my best to wipe them off on the unbloodied feathers of the bird-women's backs.

"Not sure that's any more sanitary than just leaving the blood on," he quips. "Harpies are dirty creatures."

"I'll live."

Mark shrugs. "Shame you lost that third crystal."

I slide the crystals back into my hand then walk to the edge of the roof. I spot the dead harpy lying in a broken heap not far from the asylum door. There are murderous ghosts locked in combat all around, but they might be too busy with each other to notice me...

Mark comes over to see what I'm looking at. "Wow, a ghost in a straitjacket!" he says. "Never saw that before." Then he sees what really has my attention. "Oh shit! You're not actually thinking of going down there, are you?"

"No... well, yeah. Maybe."

"Dude! You can get crystals anywhere. You have before."

"Not like these. There's something special about them. They're red and..."

Mark raises an eyebrow. "So they're like rubies or something? Aren't you rich enough as it is?"

"No, it's not that. They're not rubies. Rocks and gems are my thing. I should know what these things are, but I don't. And they just feel..."

"What?"

"I don't know, like we're *connected* somehow. You think Tartarus has gems and stones we don't have on Earth?"

Mark frowns. "Sure, I guess... Look, man... Shouldn't we be—I don't know—running for our lives? I mean, the river's right there!" He jerks his thumb over his shoulder.

"In a minute... I found these crystals when Herophilos sent me shopping for your operation."

"Ritual."

"Whatever."

"Andrus, man... We don't have time for this."

But I'm not listening. I really want that crystal, and it wants me. I can feel it, calling to me. And I'm calling to it. *With my mind, with every magic part of me.* To my surprise, the crystal flies up out of the harpy and into my outstretched hand. I stare at it dumbly, then burst into a surprised grin.

"Um, what just happened?" Mark asks. "Am I hallucinating, or did you just make that crystal fly back to you?"

"Yeah," I say. "I kind of just did."

"OK, that was freaking badass, and I want to talk to you about it—I really do—but not here, all right? Let's go."

I nod, sliding the third crystal under my skin, feeling it meld into me. I feel whole again.

WE MAKE GOOD TIME jumping from roof to roof, though there is the inevitable moment where Mark miscalculates and I have to save him from plunging to his death. Other than that, it's almost fun. Except for the whole running for our lives thing.

More harpies converge, dive bombing us. It reminds me of the Cliffs of Pain, but it also reminds me of my daydreams... the ones where I was Cronus scaling Mount Olympus out for revenge. Even though we're on top of a building in the middle of a city, it's still made of stone. In a way, it's a mountain and I remember my mantra...

I am the mountain.

I am one with it.

I am one with the earth.

I draw on my connection to power my fight. I take on more of the harpies so Mark doesn't have to. Sure, he could let Ares take over and help in the fight, but they're both still recovering. Besides, they're just harpies.

Just harpies? When did I think of any monster as "just a monster" and not a threat? After everything I've been through—everything I've fought—it makes sense. I know what harpies can do, know how they fight, and can anticipate their moves. I also know I can kill them. So now when I see them, my initial response isn't terror, but resignation.

Them again.

As we leap between roofs, I catch glimpses of centaurs and

cyclopes in the streets below, some oblivious, some attempting to follow. They don't frighten me much either, for the same reason the harpies don't.

I can beat them.

Even Captain Nessus, my old enemy, does not inspire the fear he used to. He'll be tougher than the rest, no doubt, but I can still beat him.

More troubling is my half-brother, Gyges. I see him looming across the river, all fifty heads and hundred hands of him. The size of a building, the gruesome giant is too large to fit in the narrow streets of Murder Town, so he lurks outside, near one of the three bridges leading out of the city.

Gyges is tough. I only beat him before by using the terrain to my advantage, sending him plummeting off the Bridge of Burnt Souls into the flaming Phlegethon below. He should have died, but I hadn't freed Hades yet. So he didn't. Now he can.

I can kill him, and he can kill me.

Almost as if he can sense me despite the distance between us, all fifty heads swivel in our direction. All the birds, the beasts, the reptiles and insects that make up the ring of heads on top of his massive shoulders focus on me.

"Little brother!" Gyges bellows. "Come to me! Come to Gyges! Let us continue our fight..."

Mark and I exchange a worried look.

"Don't worry," I tell him, "it's not going to happen. We just won't use that bridge. There's three bridges and only one of him."

Mark licks his lips. "Yeah, but if he's set himself up guarding that one, what's waiting for us at the other two?"

"Not sure. Probably Nessus has one, the cyclopes the other."

"And the harpies," Mark reminds me. "There's always more harpies..."

"Look, man, don't worry about it. We'll make it. I know we will."

Mark hesitates. "You think or you know?"

I force a smile. "Seriously? You even need to ask? We got this! We'll bug out of here and be back to Earth in no time."

We continue jumping, resting when we have to, but never for long. Rather than harpies, we encounter a pair of ghosts on one of the rooftops. And not just any pair.

It's Blake and Brenda.

I have no idea how they found us, but here they are.

18

REVENGE

It's like Axios all over again. As if nothing's changed and we're in gym class. Only we're not, and everything has changed. For them, for us. We're not the same people we were then. Some of us aren't even people.

I know we can walk right through Blake and Brenda because they're ghosts, but the weapons they wield are real—swords and shields, just like the punishment Mr. Cross promised if we failed to climb the wall. It makes sense that Blake and Brenda would want it this way. It's all they have to look forward to, probably all they've been thinking about since they died.

Not a rematch.

Revenge.

"You're not getting away," Blake growls, "not this time."

"Blake," I say, "Brenda... We don't have to do this. You don't have to be here, trapped in Murder Town. You can leave any time you want."

"Liar!" Blake snarls. "You think just because you got to walk away from the wall, you get to walk away from us? It's your fault we're dead! Your fault we're cursed to spend eternity in this hell."

"You cursed yourself." Mark and I draw our blades.

Blake steps forward. "I'm going to enjoy gutting you, Andrus. You always were a pussy. Now you'll be a dead one, like Brenda. Maybe I'll make you saw your legs off every day too." He grins. "You can be a matched set. My little money-makers. Maybe then you'll learn how to beg."

He's goading us into a fight—a fight we don't have time for. But Blake doesn't scare me, not after fighting Gyges and hordes of ravenous monsters. No, what scares me is the time we're wasting, and how badly I want to unleash my rage on this jackass. For all the years of torment he caused me in school, and for the eternity of torment he's so gleefully inflicting on Brenda and anyone else in this town he can get his hands on.

"You were a bully in life, Blake. Why be one in death? Why not move on?"

"I'll move on when you're dead," he replies. "What I need is payback. You got me killed. Now I'll return the favor."

I glance over at Mark, who's ready to fight. Then I look at Brenda, who also looks ready, but there's something else going on. Something behind her eyes that tells me she's wavering. That's why I'm letting Blake talk. Because maybe—just maybe—I can give him enough rope to hang himself with...

"I've been learning a lot here," Blake says. "How to hurt, how to kill. If there's one thing this place is great for, it's that."

"You shouldn't have come," Brenda says, "this place is for the dead. No mortals allowed."

"Who says I'm mortal?"

Brenda gapes. "What? You're lying!"

"It's true," Mark says. "Andrus is a Titan. And not just any Titan, but the son of Cronus. He's not human. He never was. That's why you couldn't beat us then, and that's why you can't beat us now."

Blake snorts in disbelief, but Brenda just stares. She says, "If you're the son of Cronus, why are the monsters after you?"

"Because I'm going to overthrow my father."

"We already freed Hades," Mark adds. "You wouldn't be here if we hadn't. You'd still be stuck as zombies back in Othrys."

Brenda says, "Can you put in a good word for us with Hades?"

"Shut up, Brenda," Blake says. "Don't listen to that Loser! We came to kill, didn't we? We came to make them pay!"

Brenda nods.

"All right, this is our moment. Let's slaughter these fools!"

They start forward, but Brenda lags a step behind as if unsure. Mark and I raise our weapons. Blake comes at me, and it's then I see his blade is coated with some sort of rancid oil. *Poison.* It must be. Brenda's blade is too. This changes things. I might be immortal, but I can still be killed... I'm just not sure by what. But whatever it might do to me, poison can definitely kill Mark.

I dodge Blake's first blow, and we lock blades. His perfect pretty boy face is clenched in a hateful grimace. He's close enough to see the veins bulging in his neck. His eyes are mad, staring things.

"Titan or not," Blake spits, "I'm still going to murder you!" He pushes me backward with his shield. His hate makes him strong.

I slide back toward the edge of the roof. *One step. Two.* The long fall to the street mere inches away.

Blake laughs, nasty and cruel. "You're so dead! I can't wait to get the reward that centaur promised."

"What reward?"

His eyes glitter. "I'm going to be the mayor of Murder Town! This whole place is going to be mine, and every day, I'm going to hurt you. I'm going to make you my ghost-bitch, just like Brenda."

"Why do you do that to her?" I demand. "She doesn't deserve that shit!"

"Sure she does. She likes it. *She likes being my bitch.* My little begging bitch! You know what? You're going to like it too. You and Mark both."

"You always were an asshole," I tell him. "Now you're just insane."

We fight, blades ringing. *Cut. Thrust. Parry. Chop.*

Over Blake's shoulder, I see Mark and Brenda clash, and wonder if Mark will summon Ares. But I only have a split second to wonder, and less than that to watch what happens next. I put all my attention on Blake. I hear the smash of shields, hear the thud of a body going down, but I can't tell if it's Mark or Brenda because everything I have is focused on pushing back against Blake, who's trying to knock me off the roof with his shield.

"You had everything," he hisses. "Now, I'll make sure you have nothing! Nothing but pain and death and—"

Blake tries to say the word "torture" but only manages to get half of it out before a blade punches through his heart. He stares at the metal tip in surprise, all the hate flowing out of him, all the strength and fury.

I push him away. It's then that I see it wasn't Mark who stabbed him. It was Brenda. Mark is off to my left, trying to regain his feet.

I say Brenda's name, but she doesn't hear me. She just runs Blake through again, this time through the spine and out his stomach. Blake collapses, spilling intestines.

"Why?" I ask. "Why'd you help us?"

She shrugs. "I got tired of being his bitch."

I smile.

"You really are a Titan?" she asks.

"Yeah."

"And you're going to win?"

"Yeah, we are... Eventually."

"OK," she says. There's an awkward moment of silence. I try to fill it by saying her name, but she shakes her head.

"You guys should go. Now, while you still can."

"What about you?"

Brenda smiles, not quite sane, but not half as lost as she was. "Just got to tie up a few loose ends, then I'm out of here. I can do that, right? I can leave? You weren't lying?"

"You're as free as you want to be. You always were."

Brenda stands over Blake, blade dripping with ghost-gore. "You don't want to see what happens next," she says. "Part of me doesn't want to either."

"And the other part?" I ask.

She grins. "The other part can't wait."

"You know that's the part that's keeping you here."

"I know. So I'll let it keep me here a few more minutes, then I'll be gone."

"You don't have to—" I begin.

"I know. *I want to.* Call it closure. Now go get some of your own."

"Good luck."

"You too."

Mark and I leave her there. After we jump to the next roof, I look back and see Brenda chopping off Blake's legs, but she doesn't stop there.

19

YOU ONLY LIVE ONCE... MAYBE TWICE

"All right," I tell Mark. "This looks like a good spot." We've left Blake and Brenda behind and are a lot closer to the river and to one of the three bridges leading out of Murder Town.

"You think Brenda will be all right?" Mark asks.

"Yeah. Yeah, man. I think she will."

He looks over the ledge to the street some forty-feet below. "Damn! That's a long way down."

"Well, what did you expect? It was a long way up."

Mark cracks a grin. "Maybe heights aren't my thing."

"The next building over is too far to jump, so unless we want to back track and try to angle around and hope for something better... this is it. Besides, I don't see any monsters around, and there aren't many ghosts."

"Not that we can see," Mark replies. "I don't know why, but I've got a bad feeling about this."

"This whole town gives me bad feelings. Like I said, there's no monsters. No doubt there'll be some stationed by the bridge, but..." I look over my shoulder to the opposite end of the city, expecting to see Gyges. He's not there. "Damn it!" I mutter.

"What?" Marks asks. "Andrus, what is it?"

"Nothing. Come on, the trickiest part of the descent is getting into position... Let me climb over the side and get a good grip. I'll tell you when to come down."

Once I'm in position with my hands and boots firmly planted in the wall, I tell Mark to climb down over me and grab on to my shoulders. I brace myself for the extra weight, but I what I don't prepare myself for is the death grip Mark's arm delivers as it snakes around my throat. I can't breathe, and he can't let go.

We begin to slide, my fingers losing traction in the wall, my magic failing as we descend faster and faster. *Ten feet. Twenty.* I dig my boots into the wall and reach into the stone with all my strength. It takes another ten feet before we slow to a safe speed, then stop.

Now that we're not so high and not moving so fast, Mark loosens his arm from my neck. I suck in a massive breath, feeling my magic replenish itself.

"Better?" Mark asks.

I grunt something that sounds like "Yes," and continue our descent. Mark lets go when we're about five feet off the ground. I hang there a second to give him time to get out of the way, then drop to the street.

"What about Charon?" Mark asks. "How do we know which bridge he'll be at?"

"Good point. I thought Shadow would have caught up with us by now. He should know which bridge we want."

"I don't think it's a matter of which bridge we want, but which one we're going to get," Mark says.

"True..." I check the sky for signs of Hannah's familiar, but all I get are the shrill sounds of harpies in the distance. The ghosts I saw earlier are gone, the street empty, save for us. Everything is quiet. *Too quiet.*

"Hey," I whisper to Mark as we head toward the closest bridge. "You know that bad feeling you have?"

"Yeah?" he whispers back.

"I've got it too." I draw my sword and Mark draws his. We keep moving forward, daring backward glances every few feet in case we're being flanked.

"Andrus..."

"Yeah?"

"Did you hear something?"

"What?"

"I don't know... Just for a second, I thought I heard hooves."

"Shit! I heard it too. I was hoping I'd imagined it." For a moment, I flashback to when we met the Night Patrol, the centaurs who scour the streets of Othrys after dark. Looking for curfew breakers. Looking for skulls to smash and fresh brains to devour.

"Andrus?"

"Yeah, dude?"

"We're not gonna make that bridge, are we?"

I can smell it now, the rank scent of centaur: the savage goat-men. There's another quick clatter of hooves on stone, a low bestial murmur, and now it's not just in front of us, it's behind us too. That leaves one choice.

Another alley.

"RUN!" I shout and take off, Mark keeping pace a fraction of a step behind me.

Now the sound of centaurs isn't muted but erupts into violent cries of battle. The thunder of hooves follows us into the narrow, twisting alley.

Over my shoulder, I see Captain Nessus, his brothers, and more charging after us.

"Let's hope this leads somewhere," Mark gasps.

It does. It leads to a dead end.

"Andrus! Andrus Eaves!" The gravelly voice of Captain Nessus rings out from further back. "The chase is over! There's nowhere to run. Surrender, and we will take you to your father."

"What about Mark?"

"Mark dies, you live. Those are my orders."

"And if I refuse?"

My threat is met with braying laughter. "Then you die too!"

"Yeah," I mutter to myself. "That's not gonna happen."

"What are we gonna do?" Mark asks.

I look up at the wall. Mark follows my gaze and understands what we have to do. He doesn't look happy about it.

"What if they attack us while we're climbing?" he asks.

I sheathe my sword and kneel down.

"They won't."

"What? How are you going to stop them?"

"I've got an idea." I dig my fingers into the cobblestones and pull up a chunk of the street. One stone, two, four, a dozen, then I lose count. There must be at least fifty stones in a pile at my feet.

"That's your idea? You're going to throw rocks at them?"

"No, just one." I use my earth magic to meld the rocks together, rolling them into a massive molten ball. I start pushing it, putting my back into it, building momentum. Then it's rolling on its own, like some demented bowling ball, like the severed heads I saw in the park.

I don't wait to hear the screams. I run to the dead end and wait for Mark to climb on. As soon as he's aboard, we begin our ascent. Once we're high enough, I crane my neck to see the red-hot boulder I made is blocking the alley. The centaurs won't be able to get through.

I worry about harpies since we're vulnerable while climbing, but none come. It's a good thing the harpies and centaurs hate each other and only grudgingly work together. Nessus must have had his beast-men guarding this bridge, while the harpies flew reconnaissance and guarded another.

Gyges himself kept watch on the third bridge... or at least, that's where the Lesser Titan was the last time I saw him. You'd think I would have heard him lumbering around if he was changing position. That worries me. How does a fifty-foot monstrosity hide in plain sight?

When we get to the top of the wall, we get lucky. This isn't just another building, this is the actual wall that surrounds the city. There's a crenellated parapet that runs along the far side for defenders to take cover behind. I peer over the battlements to the

Acheron below. A moat of blood, the River of Woe flows around the walls before carrying on downstream.

"You're not thinking of climbing down, are you?" Mark asks.

"No, I was thinking of jumping."

"What?" Mark sputters. "Are you serious? Why? Charon's not even down there!"

"He's not up here, either—and he won't be. At least down there, we could swim for shore, figure things out from there."

"What about the centaurs?"

"The bridges are broken, and I don't see any boats, so Gyges must have carried them across. It'll take him just as long to take them back across the moat."

"He's got a hundred hands, Andrus! How long do you think that will take him?"

"Not too long, I guess."

"Exactly! And what about the harpies? What if they come after us while we're swimming?"

"Good point. That would suck."

We walk along the parapet, checking for Charon. We're moving toward the bridge. I figure Nessus pulled all or most of his troops back from it when he thought he had us cornered. Though enough time has passed that they could have returned.

It's a gamble... Do we climb or jump down here or head for the bridge and hope Charon is waiting?

Far off, over the bridge between the one we're headed toward and the one Gyges was at, there's a flurry of harpies.

"They're after something."

Mark shrugs. "I'm just glad it's not us."

Then it hits me: *Shadow.* The harpies must be after Hannah's familiar. But what is her raven doing over there? Is that where Charon is, and can we even get there?

The bridge is ahead. We can see it now. There's activity on it: centaurs and cyclopes milling about. And below, there's Charon! The living mummy pilots his bone-encrusted boat down the bloody river as the monsters hurl rocks, spears, and more than a few insults.

They all bounce off, thanks to the invisible shield that surrounds his boat.

"Let's wait till he gets closer," I tell Mark, "then jump."

He sighs. "Have I ever told you how much I hate your plans?"

"All the time."

"Well, it's true, man. This might be your worst one yet."

"The river's deep enough."

"How do you know?"

"I just know."

"Yeah, that doesn't work for me. I just got brought back to life, and you've got me running all over Murder Town doing crazy shit, and now you want me to jump off *this* wall into *that* blood?"

"Pretty much."

He sighs louder. "OK."

"OK?"

"Yeah," he says. "You only live once... maybe twice."

Charon drifts closer. Finally, his bone-covered boat is close enough.

"Ready?" I tense for the dive.

"No," Mark says, "but yeah. I'll do it. Only you better not have to being me back to life again."

I start to make a clever reply, but hear flapping and squawking coming from behind. I look over my shoulder and see Shadow winging toward us, a flock of harpies hot on his tail. There's no more time. The only thing left to do is to jump.

As I spring into motion, Mark cries, "No, wait!"

That's when I notice something moving under the surface. *Something big.* But it's too late.

Gyges rises from the scarlet wash with an triumphant roar, all hundred hands and fifty heads flailing and gnashing. But it's not the forty-nine heads growing out of his shoulders that concerns me. It's the leech-like mouth in his belly, the nightmare fiftieth "face" ringed by eight spider-black eyes. It opens, yawning wide, yearning to devour me...

20

EATEN ALIVE

THERE'S NO TIME TO THINK, no time to scream. Into the giant's belly I go, past the purple gums with the inward sloping fangs. Right into the gullet. I've been swallowed, hungrily sucked inside the gruesome darkness.

My crystal claws spring out, punching into the tender flesh to stop my fall. I plant my boots on the contracting windpipe to finish the job. It's not easy to hold on because of all the mucous. My boots keep slipping, forcing me to reposition my feet to maintain my purchase.

I hang awkwardly as Gyges swallows, attempting to clear the blockage. Once the first tremor passes, I draw my sword. It's not easy to do with my off-hand because I can't use my right. My claws are the only thing keeping me from sliding deeper into the giant's innards.

But maybe that's where I need to be...

I look up, see the mouth—and my escape—is too far to climb. That leaves one choice. I plunge the blade into the soft tissue of Gyges' throat, then yank my claws from the mucous-strewn mess and wrap both hands around the hilt of my sword. I brace myself.

Gyges swallows again, harder. This time I don't fight. I don't try to hang on. Instead, I tug my blade down, riding it like a carving knife, like a gigantic zipper opening my enemy from within.

Everything gets hazy after that.

Hades was right. I'm reckless. Impulsive. And I may just have gotten myself killed. The worst part is, I'm supposed to die... to sacrifice myself in order to defeat Cronus. That's what the prophecy said, but I don't think it meant I should sacrifice myself here, not like this.

I lash out with my sword as I land in the giant's stomach—a foul pit roiling with acid, burning with the juices of hell. I'm swimming, trying to keep my head above the cannibal soup, lost in the steaming heat of being eaten alive. Then I remember I've done this before.

In Cronus.

Before I became who I am, what I am. When I was nothing more than a rock. So maybe I can't die here, not this way. It's something to think about as the blackness closes in.

21

DEATH OF A TITAN

Thump. Thump. I wake to a rocking motion and the sound of something impacting overhead.

Thump. It comes again.

My head hurts. My neck hurts. Hell, everything hurts! I open my eyes slowly, catching a fluttering motion though my lashes. When the harpy shrills, I come fully awake and sit up. That makes the world spin, and the shrieking harpies spin with it.

I'm lying in the bottom of a boat. I can tell it's Charon's by the skeletal decorations and by the grim Ferryman of Souls standing at the bow, working the pole that steers us downstream. Mark is here too, and Shadow. Safe, all safe, though I've felt better. Mark is covered in blood, but then so am I. It's not ours—at least I don't think it is. It's the river. The Acheron.

We're being pursued by harpies, but they can't break through the invisible shield that protects Charon's boat. That was them I heard thumping against the shield.

I have no idea how I got here. I risk sitting up again, and this time I wait for my head to clear before trying to make sense of things.

Behind us, I see the serrated skyline of Murder Town, with its skull-like domes and knife-edged towers. I see centaurs and cyclopes on the broken bridge to nowhere. And I see Gyges, my half-brother, crashing and convulsing on his back in the blood-river. How much of the river is his blood now?

The hundred terrible arms claw at the air, the fifty awful faces gurgle and moan in a chorus of doom. As I watch, the Lesser Titan sinks. Gyges sinks below the current and accepts the gift.

The Gift of Death.

As he dies, the last of the harpies gives up, reeling back toward the city. I watch her go. I watch the river. I watch my life drift by, my past, my future. And I know something's changed. In me. To me. For me and the world.

"You all right?" Mark asks.

I have to think about that before I answer. "Yeah, I think so."

But am I? I almost died.

I'm supposed to die.

But not yet, not yet... if I believe in prophecy. I'm not sure I do. Not sure I can trust Hades, and that means I'm not sure I can trust Ares, or Charon, or Hannah and Shadow... maybe even Mark, now that he's Ares' priest and they share the same body, the same "temple of the flesh."

I don't know I can trust them, but I do know I need them. That's enough. For now. I let the gentle rocking motion of the boat soothe my jangled nerves, as I lie there half in wonder, half in shock. I rub at my aching neck and shoulders, trying to work the kinks out. After a while, I ask Mark, "What happened?"

He shrugs. "I went in after you. Well, Ares and me... Ares, mostly."

"I thought you said he needed more time to rest?"

"He does! He did... you just didn't give it to him."

"I didn't know what else to do. Is Ares OK?"

"He's resting."

"You should be too."

"We all should," Mark says. "But I had to stay awake to make sure you were all right."

I shrug out of my backpack and use it as a pillow to prop my head up. "Thanks. You know, you didn't have to dive in after me."

He grins. "Of course I did! That's what heroes do... at least in all the myths and legends I heard."

We settle in to rest as our boat glides into a fog bank, leprous gray mist creeping over the red river. We're about to teleport, fading from the Acheron to the Styx, the River of Hate and Promises. From there, it's back to Earth, to the city of Othrys and the New Greece Theocracy. To rescue Mark's sister, Lucy, and my adopted parents from the Temple of the Unblinking Eye. To put a stop to Cronus and his priests. And maybe, just maybe, for me to die...

It's all so mad, so utterly insane, that I almost have to laugh. I would, if it didn't hurt so much. My body is bruised, my muscles are screaming. And my mind... well, it's seen better days too.

22

PUSHING OUR LUCK

"Maybe we shouldn't go back to Earth." I can't believe the words are coming out of my mouth, but there they are, reckless and strange.

Mark looks at me in shock. "What?"

"I mean, not right away. Hear me out: Time flows differently in the Underworld. Slower, right?"

"Right…"

"So we haven't been gone that long. That's good. I mean, that's what Hannah said, right?"

Mark nods. "Andrus, we have to go back! We have to save Lucy, and what about your parents?"

"I know it's a crazy idea, but what if we could end this now?"

"End it?" he asks. "End it how?"

"What if we went to Lake Cocytus? To Hades' castle. We could end this war! All we have to do is kill Cronus."

"You're right," Mark says.

"I am?"

"Yeah. You are crazy."

"I know. It's just…" I bite my lip, not sure how to say it.

"Just what?"

I shrug and stare at the bottom of the boat. "Never mind. It's stupid."

"No, tell me," Mark insists.

"It'd all be over. Everyone would be safe. Not just your sister, not just my parents. Everyone."

Mark chews on this while Shadows paces back and forth on the bench next to him, shaking his head.

"I know it's not Hades' plan, I know it's not what we said we'd do..."

"It's not," Mark agrees. "Look, I get what you're saying. I get where you're coming from, but we already did one reckless thing today, and there's such a thing as pushing our luck, you know?"

"But think of it! Think how famous we'd be if we killed two Titans in one day."

"We wouldn't be famous, man. *We'd be dead*. Frankly, I'm in no hurry to be a ghost again."

"I might be one soon."

Mark's expression softens. "Wow. You jump in one Titan's mouth and suddenly you've got a death wish."

"It's not that. While Herophilos was operating on you, I had a visit from Hades."

"You did? Why didn't you tell me?"

"You were out of it, there wasn't a good time, and..."

"And what?"

"I wasn't sure I should. He said there's some ancient prophecy about me. That I'm going to defeat Cronus, but the only way I can do it... The only way is for me to sacrifice myself. Maybe that's here, maybe that's now."

"It's not," Mark says. The boat rocks against the black current. Shadow perches himself on the prow and begins to preen.

Mark opens his mouth to say something, the closes it and furrows his brow. Finally, he says, "Do you have a copy of it? The prophecy?"

I reach into my backpack and hand him the scroll. "It's in some ancient Greek, shit I can't read. You're the scholar."

Mark unrolls it, furrowing his brow as he puzzles over the text. "It's a messed-up old dialect, that's for sure."

"But you can read it?"

"Mostly. The problem is, like a lot of prophecies, the wording is vague. It's open to interpretation."

"I don't know. 'Death' and 'sacrifice' seem pretty clear to me."

"Taking them literally is one way to interpret it."

"There's another?"

Mark frowns at the scroll, then rolls it up. "Mind if I hang on to this?"

"Sure."

"Thanks. I'd like to study it some more. There are some books at the Great Library in Othrys that might help translate it. Does Hannah know?"

"No. Hades told me not to tell her."

"Why not?" You told me."

"Yeah, but... he just doesn't, all right?" The truth is, I don't know how Mark is going to take the news I've fallen for Hannah after being almost in love with Lucy. I don't want to hurt him anymore than I want to hurt his sister. It occurs to me maybe I'm not good with certain emotions... processing or expressing them. Love is more complicated than hate.

"I'm sorry," Mark says. "Sorry you've been carrying this prophecy around. It must have been weighing on you."

"I'm OK."

"Dude! You're not. 'OK' is the last thing any of us are after all the shit we've been through. Seriously."

I force a smile. "Fine. I admit it: I'm messed up."

"Now you're talking," Mark jokes. "You know what the worst part is?"

"No clue. Every time I think I know, someone pulls the rug out from under me."

He laughs. "Me too! But right now, for me, the worst part is, as much as I want this all to be over, there's a part of me—a messed-up part—that never wants it to end, you know?"

"I know."

"I mean, it beats sitting in Mrs. Ploddin's history class, or climbing that damn wall in gym. And it beats coming home to that shack every night and waking up in it. Sometimes... Sometimes I can still hear my mom, scolding me. I can still see her drinking too much. Is it wrong to miss her?"

"No."

"I do and I don't. I know she must be dead now that we freed Hades. I know she must be down here in Tartarus somewhere... This whole time, I've been afraid of running into her. What she'd do, what I'd say. In a way, I'm glad we didn't run into her... I've been thinking about that a lot, especially after Blake and Brenda."

I nod, not sure what to say. Mark's mom was horrible, but she was still his mother, and I don't blame him for loving her, hating her, and whatever else he's feeling now. "I'm just glad we didn't run into Lucy, but not for the same reason. I think it means she's not dead. Same with my parents. It gives me hope there's still time to save them."

"Not if we go to fight Cronus," Mark says. "Besides, what happened to your idea to look for Prometheus or other Titans we could use as allies?"

I look up at Charon, who makes a point of not looking back. The undead ferryman keeps his empty gaze on the Styx, the black water that carries us back to Earth.

Shadow cocks his head, interested. When I don't say anything, the raven yawns and pretends to go to sleep.

I'm not sure I should talk about Prometheus or the other Titans in front of them. They might tell Hades, and the Death God might not like that. So I shrug and say, "I don't know. I've kind of given up on that idea. It's about as smart as going after Cronus now, and it'd be even more work."

I want to tell Mark about my dream, about what Cronus said about Hades, but not in front of Charon and Shadow. It's one thing to toss around different ideas that might benefit their boss and another to question his integrity. So I keep it to myself, hoping there'll be an opportunity to talk about it with Mark privately... Not that anything with Mark is private now that Ares is in him again. But what Cronus said affects the War God too, so I think it'll be safe to bring it up... Once we get back to Earth.

23

ONE-WAY TICKET

EARTH ISN'T HOW I REMEMBER IT. As we arrive in the secret underground cave beneath Bronson Canyon, it's obvious what Hades' freedom has done. The cave isn't secret anymore. The riverbank is teeming with the dead. Ghosts of every size, age, and color. They were all zombies, all cursed with immortality until now. They wait patiently for Charon, for their one-way ticket to Tartarus. Some appear confused, others relieved, a few fearful.

In what must have been mere hours ago, they were trapped in their own damaged or badly-aged bodies. Now they are free. Some murmur, others moan, but most are silent. As silent as the grave they thought they'd never see. Now here they are.

Ghosts.

As we approach, the sight of Charon's boat excites the former zombies. They point and clap and cry. *The afterlife is real.* They don't have to be trapped in this world anymore. It's a beautiful thing, watching the dead fill with hope, with the certainty their time of misery and despair is done.

Only it isn't.

Hades has a plan for them that doesn't include eternal rest and reward—they just don't know it yet.

I scan the crowd for people I know: for my adopted parents, for Lucy. I don't see them. That means they're still alive... Although maybe not. Maybe they've already been sacrificed to Cronus and are being digested in his stomach, as I almost was, and almost was again in Gyges.

There is another possibility... they could have already died and moved on, somehow found their way into the Underworld like Blake and Brenda. How did Blake and Brenda get to Murder Town so fast? They were always resourceful in life, so I suppose anything is possible... Still, it bothers me.

The dead lose all track of time, so them acting like they'd been in Murder Town for days or weeks, maybe even months sort of makes sense. It probably felt like that to them. That place, that terrible place! It has an effect on your mind, your soul. It weighs it down, makes even the maddest idea seem sane. I should know—I had a few of my own down there, and not just in Murder Town.

As our boat pulls up alongside the riverbank, the ghosts rush forward, desperate to board. But they can't. The force field stops them, and I know no coin or gem can buy them passage. Not until Hades has won.

"What are they supposed to do?" I ask Charon, knowing the cobweb-crusted boatman can't answer me—not in any way I can hear. Still, I persist. "You'll tell them, won't you? You'll let the dead know about Hades' plan and their part in it?"

The mummy nods, his bleached and bearded face free of pity, free from any emotion. Whatever Charon feels—*or doesn't*—lies hidden behind those empty sockets. He points to the shore, to the tunnel back to the surface. His jaw clacks open, exhaling a puff of dust.

That must be a signal. Shadow caws and flies off, eager to scout ahead.

"Thanks," I tell Charon. "You really saved us back there. We won't forget that."

Again, the ferryman nods. Again, he points, his bony finger telling us this part of our adventure is over, and the next is about to begin.

24

A GENERAL USES EVERY WEAPON

THE TUNNEL TO THE SURFACE has been cleared, no doubt so Nessus and the rest of the Night Patrol could pursue us into Tartarus. I'm glad I don't have to waste time digging through it, spending magic I'd rather save for dealing with Inquisitor Anton and the rest of the priests.

The tunnel is still filled with the toxic fumes of Tartarus. Once we're through it and out into the lower cave, the fumes clear. I can tell by the way my chest tightens and how I cough, expelling the last of the deadly vapors. Clean air fills my lungs. *Earth air.* It takes me a moment to adjust, then I'm fine.

"It's safe," I tell Mark. "You can take your ghost-mask off."

He removes the strange device made of mist and "rolls" it up, stuffing it into his belt pouch. "Fresh air!" he says, then wrinkles his nose in disgust. "Well, maybe not so fresh. I can still smell that rotten egg stink from the underworld, and... *ugh!* What's that? Monsters too?"

I step around a pile of centaur droppings. "Yeah, but they're not here now."

"Good thing. They probably posted some guards in the Canyon though. We need to be ready."

I pop my claws out. "I'm always ready."

Mark snorts. "Easy, tough guy. Let's not get into any fights we don't have to."

"Really? I thought you'd be more gung-ho now that you're a priest of Ares."

"Yeah, well... Old habits. For now, let's just say I'm focused more on military tactics and strategy..." His gaze falls on a patch of ground at the bottom of the cliffs leading to the upper passage—the tunnel that will take us back to the surface. "Hey, you remember that spot? That's where I fell the day you brought me here to train for that gym challenge. Right over there..."

I sheathe my claws. "I remember."

"Cracked my skull wide open! Would have been a zombie if it hadn't been for Hannah and Herophilos." He sighs. "I still ended up dead though."

"Well, you're not, and you won't be again. Not for a long time."

"Right over there," Mark mutters, still staring at the spot. "Should have known, should have seen it coming..." He chuckles in resignation. "Life sure is funny. A few days ago, we were just a couple of regular guys. Not friends, not even acquaintances. We went to the same school, but lived in different worlds. Now look at us: best buddies, heroes. It's crazy!"

I smile but don't reply. I need a minute to bring up the thing we need to talk about. *Hades.* His plan, and what it means for us and humanity.

Mark can tell something's off. He sees the pain behind my smile. "Andrus? What's wrong? You're not worried about rescuing Lucy and your parents, are you? Because we just fought our way through hell and back. Those priests won't stand a chance!"

"It's not that. I mean, of course I'm worried about saving our families in time, but there's something else. I couldn't tell you before and I'm not sure we'll have another chance, so it has to be now."

"Didn't we already have this conversation in the boat? Look, after we pull off the rescue, I'll get those books from the library and translate the prophecy. It'll be fine."

"This isn't about the prophecy—not directly."

"It isn't?" He frowns. "Then what do you need to talk to me about?"

"Back in Murder Town, while you were being operated on, Hades came and told me about the prophecy. That's the part I told you in the boat."

"So what didn't you tell me?"

I sigh. "Right after Hades left, I fell asleep and had a dream. Not just any dream. It was real. I was in Lake Cocytus, drowning, sinking below the ice, just like when Hades imprisoned the Titans... Cronus warned me that Hades was using me, that he was using all of us, including Ares, and there's a reason Zeus and Poseidon made Hades the God of Death. Cronus said Hades only knows how to rule the dead, not the living."

"So he'll learn," Mark says. "Big deal."

"What if he doesn't want to? What if, after the Titans are defeated, Hades kills everyone instead?"

"Why would he do that?"

"Because then he doesn't have to learn, doesn't have to grow. He doesn't have to do anything except what he's always done. And thanks to the prophecy, I'll be dead, so I can't stop him."

"It's not true," Mark says, but I can see the doubt wrestling behind his eyes.

I shrug. "Maybe Cronus lied. Maybe he didn't. But if everyone is dead, Ares won't have anyone left alive to worship him, not even you! He'll never be able to fully recover and Hades will be able to kill him and rule unopposed. Who'll be left to rebel against him then? The dead?"

Mark's eyes flare red-gold, so I know I've got Ares' attention. When Mark speaks, it's not as himself. It's as the God of War, his voice deeper, harsher. "This is a serious accusation, Andrus. Cronus is a deceiver, but sometimes the truth wounds worse than any lie. Tell me everything."

I do, though I leave out the part about me being the Bridge Between Worlds.

When I'm done, Ares nods. "I appreciate you trusting me with this information. I know it could not have been easy after all that has passed between us…"

"I'm not exactly over what you made me do—sacrificing Mark to free Hades—but I understand it. And I'm grateful to you for saving us in Murder Town and before. I know you did that at great personal cost. You risked everything for us."

Ares shrugs. "That is what allies do. They sacrifice for each other."

"No," I tell him. "That's what friends do." I hold out my hand.

The War God clasps it and gives a grim smile. "Friends, then."

"I thought War doesn't have friends?" I tease.

His smile widens. "War doesn't, but apparently, I do."

"What about what Cronus said? Was it the truth?"

"It was his version of it—or the version he wants us to hear. The thing that complicates it is not that Cronus is a deceiver, but that Hades was never well-liked among the Gods. My father, Zeus, rarely had a good word for him, but he never hated him. It was more like he didn't understand him… much like he never understood me. And that failure led to Hades and I becoming closer… Death and War, they both feast on life."

"Only War needs someone to win," I say, "and Death doesn't."

"That's one way of putting it."

"So what are we going to do? Trust Hades?"

"We're going to do what any wise general does. We're going to keep our friends close, and our enemies closer."

"How do we do that?" I ask.

"Through Hannah. She is Hades' daughter, and closer to him than any of us. She is also in love with you."

"She is?" I blurt.

Ares shakes his head. "Andrus, I am the God of War, not the God of Love, but I am not blind. I see what I see, I know what I know."

"I don't want to use her."

"*Then you are not ready to win.* A general uses every weapon at his disposal… and love… love is the most powerful." Ares cocks his head toward the cliffs. "Shadow is returning. Do not speak of your suspicions in front of the raven. The bird reports not only to Hannah, but to Hades as well. Anything it hears, Hades hears. Anything it sees..."

"Hades sees," I finish for him.

"We will talk again, Andrus."

"What about the upcoming fight? Can we count on you?"

"No. I expended most of my energy in Murder Town. It would be... unwise to call on me again in combat. I must sleep."

"All right. So when can we call on you?"

"Soon..." His red-gold eyes fade, returning to Mark's normal color as Shadow flies into the cave. The bird flaps excitedly, trying to tell us something, but now that Mark's not a ghost, he doesn't speak raven anymore. Then I get an idea.

"Are there monsters guarding the exit?" I ask the familiar. "Caw once or yes, twice for no."

Shadow caws once.

"Centaurs?"

He caws again.

"Harpies?"

Another caw.

"Anything else?"

Two caws.

"Monsters, huh?" Mark says. "I told you there'd be guards."

"Don't worry. We can sneak out during the shift change, when the Day Patrol takes over. There won't be harpies then or centaurs, just ordinary warriors... What about it, Shadow? Is it almost dawn?"

The bird caws once.

"Clever," Mark says. "We should have set up this communication system sooner."

"Yeah, well, we thought of it now..." And then another idea hits me. Only to pull it off, we're going to need Hades' help.

25

WE DIDN'T SAVE YOU

I tell my plan to Shadow, who promptly teleports away in a puff of black smoke and feathers.

"Think it'll work?" Mark asks.

"As long as Hades comes through for us."

"Why wouldn't he?" Mark says, then adds, "Oh... right. Because you don't trust him."

"You heard my conversation with Ares?"

"More or less. It's kind of like listening to someone when you're half-asleep. The parts I don't get, Ares fills me in on later. But back to Hades... you really think he'll kill everyone?"

"Maybe. That's where I get into the not trusting him part. But helping us out now before he's won? I'm confident he'll come through."

And a few seconds later, he does. A line of ghosts file up from the tunnel where we left them. They float past us, up into the higher passage that leads to the surface.

"This is some next level shit," Mark says. "You've really stepped up your strategy. I wasn't sure you were going to come back after..." He stops himself and looks away.

"After what?" I ask.

He watches the last of the ghosts drift out of sight. I know he's stalling, but I bet it's more than that. I bet some piece of him is empathizing with the dead. After all, he used to be one of them.

"Mark? What do you mean, you weren't sure I was going to come back from what?"

His shoulders sag. "Forget it, man. I was talking out my ass."

"If you know something, say it."

He looks at me. "Back in Murder Town... when I—when we, Ares and me—jumped in after you..."

"What?"

"We didn't save you, Andrus."

"What are you talking about? Of course you saved me. How else did I get here?"

Mark chews his lip. "We found you, in Gyges's stomach... only you weren't drowning, you weren't dying... you were killing him. Carving him up! Whole pieces of him were missing. And you weren't you. I mean, you weren't in control. You were in a killing rage, and you wouldn't stop, wouldn't listen..."

"So what happened?"

"We knocked you out."

I touch the back of my head. "Really? It doesn't feel like it."

"Maybe your head is made of rocks," he jokes. "Anyway, hitting you didn't work."

"What did?"

"We had to choke you out. If we hadn't, you'd still be in that Titan's stomach."

"I don't remember any of that."

"Honestly, I'm not surprised. I've seen you mad, but never like that. Never so... primal, so full of rage! It scared me. Fortunately, Ares was in charge. He knew what to do, so we did it. I wish we didn't have to, but... Well, we're here now, aren't we?"

I don't know what to say. I know I blacked out, but I didn't know it was from rage. The last thing I remember is being a rock, remembering... and somehow, maybe I reverted to that state? To becoming a primal, elemental force—something that doesn't know how to think, but only how to kill? To destroy?

"You all right?" Mark asks.

I purse my lips like I tasted something foul. "Yeah, I'm OK. I just... Well, thanks, for pulling me out of there. No matter how you had to do it."

"Is that... *that rage*... You think it's part of being a Titan? Something buried deep, or something you're evolving into?"

"Maybe, I'm not sure. I guess we'll find out."

A SHORT TIME LATER, Shadow returns to let us know it's safe to leave now. He croaks some sort of raven word for goodbye, then teleports away.

"Where do you think he's gone?" I ask Mark.

"Back to Hannah."

"Think we'll see her again?"

"Definitely," Mark replies.

Outside, we're welcomed by warm blue sky and the rising sun—the first we've seen in what feels like forever.

We walk right past the human guards. They're all possessed by ghosts now, a trick that wouldn't have worked against the centaurs and harpies since monsters have no souls.

What did Ares say? Oh yeah... '*A general uses every weapon.*' He's right. We need to use Hades now, while he's on our side, and if he isn't later... Well, we'll cross that bridge when we come to it. Cross it, burn it, crush it—whatever it takes to save humanity.

"Feels weird not to have a stone roof over our heads," I say as we walk out of Bronson Canyon into the welcoming light of a new day. "I kind of miss it."

Mark snorts. "You would, you're part-rock."

"Good point. So... got any ideas? I used all my best ones getting us here."

Mark shrugs. "Get to the temple, save the people we love and kill the people we hate. What could be simpler than that?"

I like it. Maybe a little too much. Especially the killing part.

26

IT'S EASIER TO HOPE

O THRYS IS THE CAPITAL of the New Greece Theocracy. It is built on what used to be the city of Los Angeles, in the country that used to be called the United States of America.

The Gods War changed that.

The Gods War swept the old world away, burning, blasting, and drowning what was left. The American west coast is all that remains, and it came under the control of the victors of the war—the Titans.

Led by Cronus, the Titans quickly lost interest in direct rule, ceding day to day control of their earthly dominion to the human priests of the NGT. These priests are led by an archieréas—a high priest—and his name is Enoch Vola. Under him, yet set apart from the rest of the priesthood, is the Inquisition... those who ferret out traitors, heretics, and unbelievers.

Inquisitor Anton is one of them. Anton, my enemy. Anton, who raped Mark's sister and denied Lucy her rightful scholarship to Axios... the only path out of that Loserville shack she called home.

I'm going to kill Anton. I'm going to kill him for what he did, and to make sure he never does it again. I'm going to kill Archieréas Vola and all the rest of the blue-robed maniacs in the temple. And then I'm going to tear it down, stone by stone, until nothing is left. But this isn't just a mission of vengeance, it's a rescue. The priests have my parents. They have Mark's sister...

The hardest part is not the fear I won't be able to save Lucy. The hardest part will be telling her I'm in love with Hannah. But is it love if I'm using her, like Ares suggested? Or is it something else, something I don't have words for?

It would be easier to love Lucy. Part of me still does. Part of me always will. That time we had—so short, so sweet—it was a revelation. I thought it would be enough. And then... and then Hannah came into my life, with her dark eyes and darker magic. She drew me to her. *The daughter of Hades.*

There's no way to explain it. No way Lucy can understand. She'll think it's because she's poor, because she's human, because all the other reasons she's told herself she'll never have anything good in this life. I don't want to do that to her. I don't want to be part of that. Lucy's been hurt enough as it is... but that's no reason to stay with her. And what is breaking up with her going to mean for my friendship with Mark? I think we'll survive it. I hope we will.

I don't even know why I'm thinking about this stuff now when I should be planning the mission. If the prophecy is true, then all the rest of this stuff—who I love and who I don't—won't matter. But it's easier to think about love than all the rage and ruin to come.

THE CITY HAS CHANGED. There are no more zombies shuffling around. Instead, there are sanitation crews rolling out to clean up the city's sudden crop of corpses.

The Gift of Death.

"It stinks almost as bad as Tartarus," Mark complains as we pass a pile of bodies stacked like cordwood. The sanitation crew busy themselves tossing the dead into the back of their garbage truck. The young, the old, all shapes and sizes, get tossed in by two-man teams. When the truck gets too full, they run the compactor, grinding bodies to hamburger.

"Reminds me of Murder Town," I whisper back.

Mark grunts. "Damn! Living or dead, some things never change."

"We'll change 'em." I say it like I mean it, even though the odds are against it. It's not just the Titans, or the priests, or the monsters that's the problem, it's humanity. What they do to each other, what they've always done.

As the sun climbs the ocean-blue sky, morning traffic increases. People come, people go. On foot or in cars, on their way to school, to work, or slaves running errands for their masters.

It doesn't matter who they are. They all know something is wrong. The sanitation crews, the corpses in the street, tell them the world is changing, and that change is about to come crashing down. Yet they avert their eyes and scurry on, going about their everyday tasks, ignoring the problem. It's easier to hope. To trust that things will get better, that times aren't so tough, that everything will work out if we just believe the lies the government tells us.

As Mark and I travel deeper into downtown, we notice priests stationed at important intersections, each tasked with haranguing the crowd, assuring the faithful to stay firm, that just because the zombies—the aged and infirm—are dying, it does not spell doom for them. Everything that happens is the will of Cronus, and his Unblinking Eye is always watching...

We go out of our way to avoid the priests, not wanting to be spotted, and the same goes for the familiar red and white NGT prowl cars.

After taking a few unavoidable detours, we pass the Museum of Failure. This is where zombies are artfully hung from hooks, then put on display as a warning to behave and believe in the Titans.

'This could be you,' Mrs. Ploddin told us on our field trip last year. 'This is the price you pay when you fail the NGT. It's the price you pay when you fail yourself.'

Our history teacher always was a bitch, but if I remember anything from her class, it's what she showed me on that trip. Those poor wretches, hanging there, immortal and unable to die, begging for death, for me—for anyone—to end their suffering.

All that's over now. There's a sanitation crew carting the once-living, now lifeless displays out in wheelbarrows. Into the truck. *Into the grinder.* Another crew member stands by with a hose hooked up to a hydrant, ready to wash the dripping blood from the truck and from the street.

It's working. The Theocracy is falling apart. The signs are all around. Once the citizens understand, once they choose to see, maybe then they'll be ready to rebel. After all, if they fail, they won't be put in a museum to be tortured, they'll be able to go to Tartarus and their reward. Or will they?

Not as long as Cronus and the Titans control the Underworld. Some ghosts might slip through, but others will be caught and punished. But not like Murder Town, where people choose to go and live out their darkest fantasies. If I know my father, this will be a prison—an eternal prison—and not one you can enter or leave by choice. It will be the Museum of Failure on an epic scale.

That's why we need to spread the word. We need to let people know Hades is free and the Gods War isn't over.

It's only just begun.

27

GOOD INTENTIONS

The Temple of the Unblinking Eye is a huge white building in the heart of downtown Othrys. It rises up in the ancient Greek style, supported by ornate columns. Not just a place of worship, the Temple is also a sprawling administrative complex. It is home to the high priest, Archieréas Vola, and his officials, the Great Library, and the training college for priests. The Inquisition is based here, as is the Night Patrol, though the monsters' barracks are deep underground.

Some say the Titans themselves live behind these walls, and maybe they do from time to time, but there is also a portal to Tartarus...

The sacrificial pit.

It is where those who have sinned against the state are thrown, cast down to Tartarus, straight into Cronus' stomach to be digested for eternity—or however long they last now that Death has returned to the world.

Mark and I have taken position on the roof of an apartment tower overlooking the temple. We're high enough not to be seen, but low enough to observe the comings and goings of the blue-robed priests and red-cloaked warriors. Getting past security will be tough.

I suggest tunneling our way in, but Mark warns we'd have no

idea where we'd end up. It could be on the wrong end of the complex. It could be in the barracks of the Night Patrol. To further complicate matters, this isn't the solid rock of Tartarus I'd be digging up. It's city streets and sewers, gas lines... If I screw up, if I zig when I should have zagged, I could bring an entire city block raining down on our heads. I might be able to survive that, but I can't risk the lives of my friends and family or hurting random citizens.

I could really use that Bridge Between Worlds power now so we could teleport in and out, but that's like wishing for a miracle. It's nice if it happens, but we can't count on it. You have to make your own luck.

We figure if we can pin down the schedule, we can use it to create an opportunity to infiltrate the temple. The thinking is maybe we'll fall in behind a troop of warriors on their way back from patrol. *Just march right in.* We'll need uniforms for that, but the warriors all wear red-plumed Corinthian helmets; their gold cheek plates will hide our faces.

Once we're inside, we'll make our way to the dungeon and from there, rescue our loved ones. The plan gets sketchy after that. I know I should be thinking of a solution, but instead, my mind wanders, daydreaming off as it always does, back to the past.

The last time Mark and I were here was Sunday. The day of glory, the day of worship. Archieréas Vola had whipped the faithful into a frenzy during the Ritual of the Worm, where some poor sinner had his legs sawed off by Inquisitor Anton. The newly made "worm" was forced to crawl around the temple, kicked at and spat on by the crowd, all in an attempt to prove his innocence. Unable to make a full circuit of the room, he was cast into the fiery pit. I can still see him fall, still hear him scream.

All the way down.

I'd seen it before, of course. Many times, and you'd think I'd be desensitized to it. That I might even enjoy it. I don't know why that time the ritual got to me, made me question everything. Maybe because for the first time, I saw myself in that man, that victim, that "worm." For the first time, my life was in danger. Everything was changing, careening out of control. *That worm could be me.*

In a way, it is. Like the worm, I'm being forced to run a cruel maze in a temple the size of Tartarus, the size of the Theocracy. I'm being humiliated, broken, made to do things I don't want and no one should be made to do. And no matter how far I crawl, no matter what I do, the pit is waiting.

Cronus is watching.

His hunger is real...

But I have a hunger of my own. I thought it was for justice, but one man's justice is another man's revenge. What Mark told me—what he said I was doing to Gyges, in Gyges—frightens me.

What am I becoming? I thought I knew, but the definition keeps changing... *Human. Titan. Bridge.* Now Blackout Killer, lost to primal rage. I tell myself I want to be good, to help, to love... but I also want to hurt, to hate and destroy. It's hard to reconcile these things, to live and be them.

I'm no philosopher, no sage, no great thinker. I just am, but it's difficult to simply "be" when the ground keeps shifting underfoot. First, like a tremor, warning me of change. Then an earthquake that tears my image of myself apart. Now it's like quicksand, and the more I struggle to be just one thing—*a hero*—the more I'm pulled into being something else. Manipulated by friends, by allies, and of course by Cronus. It all leads back to him. He's the voice at the bottom of the pit. He's the inexorable force sucking me under.

What if I'm becoming like him? What if all that time I spent in his belly absorbing his powers, I was also absorbing his evil? What if I'm becoming a danger? Then the prophecy makes sense. Then I should sacrifice myself rather than become a tyrant like Cronus...

I remember what one of the Inquisition's secret police told me after the ritual, a man I'd met when I'd gone to the bathroom to wash the worm's blood off my toga. He warned me, 'Some stains never come clean.' Now I know he's right. I'll never be free of the stain of my birth.

I need to die so others can live. The thing is... what kind of world will I leave behind? Will anyone be left alive if Hades wins and Cronus dies?

That's it. That's why I'm hesitating. I don't want to accept the prophecy because I don't want to accept I won't be around to make sure I didn't destroy one tyranny only to replace it with another. But isn't that what always happens? We all start with good intentions, then everything goes to shit.

Gods. Titans. Humans.

It's all the same. We're all the same.

Something needs to change. Maybe... maybe Hades is right to kill everyone. If we were all dead, we'd be free to be whatever we wanted... and have all the time in the world to enjoy it. There'd be no more wars, no more involuntary suffering.

There would be peace—the peace of the grave.

"Andrus?" Mark's voice knocks me out of my gloom and back to reality. "You've been staring at the temple a long time. You got a plan or is this one of your daydreams?"

"Sorry." I tear my gaze away from the temple. "I was just thinking about the last time we were here."

"The worm?"

I nod.

"Me too. That was the turning point. That's when everything got real."

"I'm not sure I know what real is... not anymore."

A voice from behind us says, *"I do."*

28

REUNITED

Hannah Stillwater stands behind us, hands on her hips. Shadow is with her. "Miss me?" she says in that charming sarcastic way she has. That way I've missed since we parted company what seems like forever ago. But the happiness of being reunited is tempered by my fear of her father as well as my impending sacrifice. These things combine to paralyze me when I want nothing more than to take her in my arms.

When I don't move to embrace her, Hannah shrugs. "So what's up? I see you made it out of Murder Town alive."

"We did," Mark says. "Barely! I wasn't sure we would, especially at the end. Things got... complicated."

"Oh, I like complicated. It's kind of my thing." She winks at me when she says it.

I wink back, which seems to reassure her I haven't completely fallen out of love. My emotions are all choked up, so I can't think of anything clever to say. Instead, I go with, "Dr. Herophilos sends his regards."

"Does he? He's such a sweetie." She looks Mark over. "The doc does good work."

"Actually," I say, "he prefers to be called doctor."

Hannah smirks. "Is that what he told you? I've been calling Herophilos 'doc' for years and he never corrected me."

"Maybe because you're Hades' daughter."

Shadow caws and bobs his beak, scratching impatiently at the concrete roof.

"Enough small talk. My father wants to know what your plan is."

We tell her.

When we're done, Hannah stares at us. "That's it? That's your plan?"

"Well, yeah," I say. "Sort of."

She frowns. "What do you mean, 'sort of'?"

Mark and I look at each other. We both talk at the same time, which doesn't work, so I let him go first.

"Actually, now that you're here," Mark says, "and I'm sure Andrus is thinking the same thing, um... We were wondering—hoping, really—that you could ask your father to send in his ghosts. With all the guards possessed, we could just walk right in, no problem."

"Yeah," I say. "It'd be perfect! We'd still need disguises though, in case the ghosts can't possess everyone."

Hannah sighs. "You geniuses know there are wards on the temple, right?"

"You sure?" I say. "I was really hoping there wasn't."

"Well, there are! That temple is the center of the Titans' power on Earth, so it's the most heavily-warded place on the planet."

"So... what are you saying?"

"I'm saying there's a shit-ton of wards in there! That the whole temple is covered in them, and that you can't walk five feet without stepping on one. And you can't tunnel in, if that was your next bright idea."

I try not to look guilty. "No. I mean, yeah, I considered it, but I don't know the layout well enough. Plus, I didn't want to accidentally wreck the city, so... that's why I thought the ghosts would be better."

"They would," Hannah agrees, "but the reason that won't work is not because my father would veto it, but because the wards break any possessions as soon as you enter the temple. That includes yours, Mark."

His jaw drops. "What? But no! It can't. *I have to go in.* I have to save Lucy!"

"You can't," she says. "We can."

"You have to promise," Mark says.

I hug him. "I promise. Your sister will be safe and sound. You have my word."

"Mine too," Hannah adds.

"All right," Mark says. "I guess I don't have a choice. We're going to need Ares, so I can't break the possession."

Hannah hugs Mark. "You wouldn't want to. Both of you are still recovering from your sacrifice. Neither of you are strong enough yet to live without the other. I'm sorry you can't go. I know how much this means to you."

"Thanks," Mark says. "You'll take care of Andrus for me too, right? You won't let anything happen to him?"

"Andrus can take care of himself, but yeah, I'll keep an eye on him. Don't worry. What are you going to do while we're in the temple?"

Mark shrugs. "I could set up a safe house for us to hide out after the rescue. I know Loserville like the back of my hand. There are all kinds of places to hide."

"Good," Hannah says. "That may not be as sexy as infiltrating the temple, but it's a whole lot safer."

"Couldn't Hades attack the temple?" I ask Hannah.

"Nope. Wards, remember?"

"Those are some pretty powerful wards if they can keep a God out!"

"Tell me about it," Hannah says. "It's just like how they had wards to keep my father prisoner, only in reverse—these wards keep him and all the Gods out."

"Is that why your father took you with him back in Tartarus? To teach you how to disable ultra-powerful wards?"

She nods. "It sucked missing out on all the fun with you guys, but

I learned a lot. Plus, I got to spend time with my dad, you know? I wish I could have been in two places at once. I sent Shadow to help you out. That was the best I could do."

"Thanks," I say. "Your familiar's a good scout."

Hannah grins. "He is, isn't he? Oh hey! I almost forgot... Remember how I said my father can't help attack the temple?"

"Yeah..."

"Well, that doesn't mean he can't help us *escape*. Trust me; all we have to is get in and get out. Hades will take care of the rest."

"What do you mean, 'take care of'?" I ask.

Her grin widens. "He's got ghosts possessing NGT drivers with armor-plated SUVs. Three black ones. They're standing by, ready to swoop in and pick us up. All we have to do is get out alive..."

29

WATCH OUT

Mark asks me to walk him to the elevator. I tell Hannah I'll be right back. She nods and returns to watching the temple.

As soon as we're inside the building and safely out of her and Shadow's earshot, Mark says, "I'll sneak into Axios and steal some books to help translate the prophecy. You know, like we talked about…"

"You think that'll work? I mean, do they even have the right books? I never spent much time in the library."

"Tell me about it," Mark jokes. "Anyway, I think it'll be fine. I was hoping to access the Great Library in the temple, but I guess that's not going to happen."

We walk to the elevator. Mark doesn't hit the button. He sighs and runs a hand through his hair. I let him think, waiting for him to say what he needs to say. When he finally speaks, all he says is, "Shit!"

"Hey, everything's going to be OK."

"I'm worried," he says, "not just worried about us, but about Hannah… and her dad. I'm worried they're going to play us, like they did in Tartarus. What they did, what they made us do…" He throws up his hands in a helpless gesture. "It was messed up, even if it was necessary."

"I know, but we've got Ares on our side now."

"Ares is not as strong as Hades and he's in no shape to take him on even if he were. He'll watch out for me, but you... You need to watch out for yourself."

"I will."

Mark nods. "Promise me—promise us—you won't do anything stupid."

"Who me?" I joke.

"Ha ha. Listen, man. I'm serious! Get in, get out. Keep my sister safe. And yourself."

"I'll get her out. You be careful too, all right?"

"Always." Mark hits the elevator button. "Except when I have to dive in after you."

We chuckle at the memory, but I know it's still raw underneath. The sheer horror of being swallowed alive for me, the fear of what I became for him—and what I could become again.

The elevator door opens. Mark steps in. Before it can close, I reach out a hand to stop it. "Hey, one more thing. When you're researching the prophecy..." I swallow hard, forcing myself to say it: "I need you to look up the Bridge Between Worlds."

Mark gives me a blank stare. "What's that?"

"Something Cronus called me. He says it's what I am, that I can open bridges—*portals*–to other dimensions. It's the reason he wants me to join him. He says if I do, he'll spare my friends and family."

"In return for what?" Mark asks.

"For using my power to help him conquer new worlds. That's what he told me."

"And you're just telling me this now because... why?"

I shrug. "I wanted to, but I wasn't sure I could trust Ares. Now I do."

"OK. I get it, man. So do you think you have it—this power?"

"Yeah, only I don't have any control over it... So far, it seems tied to my dreams. Like maybe those weren't daydreams I had after all, but visions of other dimensions. Only that last dream in Murder

Town... I think I really went to Lake Cocytus. Either that, or I brought part of the lake to me."

"I wondered how you got wet, but after just coming back to life, it seemed like the least of my worries."

"Thanks for not asking. That would have been awkward. Damn... If I understood my power better, then maybe I could use it, you know? But not for Cronus. I could use it for us, for our families. Either to win this war, or to get us out of here, someplace safe."

"Back when we found you in Gyges' stomach..." Marks begins, then stops himself with a frown.

"Yeah?"

"Remember how I said pieces of Gyges were missing? That you were carving him up?"

I nod, feeling uncomfortable with the memory.

"The pieces were too large for your sword or your claws. There was a lot going on at the time, so I didn't question it then, but now that you've told me about this new power..." He goes quiet and his eyes won't meet mine.

I grab him by the shoulders and shake him until he looks at me again. "What? What is it? What did I do, Mark?"

"I think maybe you were teleporting pieces of him away. I think that's how you killed Gyges. I'm not sure we could have won otherwise."

I let go of Mark and pace. "OK, that's gross, but it's good, right? I can use that against Cronus!"

"You weren't in control. You were out of your mind with rage. You couldn't recognize friend from foe. You just wanted to kill. That's why Ares and I had to knock you out. You wouldn't have stopped with slaughtering Gyges. You would have slaughtered us next."

I stop pacing. Now I'm the one who doesn't want to look at him. "No, that's not true! I would never... I'm not... not like that. I'm not evil. I'm not my father!"

"I never said you were. And I'm not saying you can never learn to control it, only that maybe your new power is rage-activated. So you should keep your emotions in check on this rescue mission. I don't want you flipping out and killing the people we're trying to save."

It takes a massive effort to meet his gaze. "I... I'll stay in control. I promise. I won't get angry. I'll stay cold, like Hades."

"Don't go cold," Mark says. "Stay cool. Anger is an energy. Either you use it, or it uses you."

"Thanks. I'll remember."

He breathes a sigh of relief. "All right. I'll ask Ares about this 'Bridge Between Worlds' thing when he wakes up. Maybe he can tell us something. Does Hannah know?"

I shake my head.

"Good," Mark says. "Keep it that way."

I tell him I will. The elevator door shuts, leaving me alone in the hallway. I feel better for telling Mark. I trust him—and Ares—not to use it against me. It's what they're going to find out I'm afraid of. That they're going to tell me I'm cursed, doomed, or worse...

30

EVERYTHING'S COMPLICATED

I join Hannah on the rooftop. I'm not sure what to do. I want to be with her, but I'm also afraid to be. Because of her father. But not just him, her loyalty to him. It's a problem, and it's not like I can come out and say, "Hey, I think you should betray your dad if he betrays us." Diplomacy was never my strong suit. People were never my strong suit.

Life was simpler before. Home and school were where I dealt with people, and then there was my alone time, amid the rocks and stones, the peace of the earth. There was safety there. Comfort. None of this pain and confusion.

Everything's complicated.

"Hey," I say to announce I'm back.

"Hey," Hannah returns the greeting. She turns slowly, cocking a dark brow. Looking at me with those dark eyes. Witch eyes that see more than they say.

I scratch the back of my head. "I'm sorry about before. For not getting up, not hugging you."

Hannah shrugs. "It's all right."

"No, it's not. I should have. I wanted to."

"But you didn't."

"No."

"Why not? Something wrong?"

I look past her, out to the city. To the sparkling skyline of glass and steel.

"You don't have to tell me," Hannah says. "I know."

I gulp awkwardly. "What? You do?"

She gets up from her kneeling position at the ledge. She comes over to me, wrapping those witchy arms around me, and staring deep into my eyes. "You're afraid."

"I am?"

"Uh-huh. Afraid of us, of everything."

I swallow, trembling at the nearness of her. The soft feel, the soft touch. "Where's your familiar?"

"I sent him to scout. He won't be back to bother us. Not until I summon him."

"Oh. Um, that's good."

"Is it?"

I nod. "Yeah."

"Tell me why."

"Why? You want to know why?"

"Yeah. Why is it good we're alone?"

I can't stop looking at her, can't stop falling into her eyes. "Because I love you. Because we might not get another chance to be alone. Because I'm afraid, like you said. Of us, of everything."

"Everything?" she teases, burying her face in my neck, pressing her lips to my skin. "Even... this?" Her head comes up, her eyes meet mine, then her lips are on me, her love in me.

I stand very still. Paralyzed. I don't breathe, find it hard to think. Hannah is here, in my arms, smelling like she does, feeling like she feels.

She's flowers in the rain.

Petal soft, petal soft.

I kiss her back. I want to do things I can't say, only feel. And yet, I can't. I can't be with Hannah, not completely. Not while there is mistrust between us. I break free of her, wrestling with this thing between us.

"What is it?" Hannah asks. "Andrus, what's wrong?"

"Us, this..." I gesture past her toward the invisible gulf between us. "When I was in Murder Town, your father came to see me."

"He told you to keep away from me."

"Something like that."

She sighs. "He told me the same. Warned me not to get involved... I never had anyone of my own before. Just the ghosts and Shadow. He thinks I'll get hurt."

"You might."

She shrugs. "Everyone gets hurt sooner or later. Maybe it's our turn. You know, on top of all the other pain. Or maybe it's our way out, a way past the pain to something beautiful, you know?"

I want to tell her about the prophecy. I want to tell her I'm going to die. I want to tell Hannah everything because I want to be her everything. Instead, I just stand there.

"Don't you think it could be beautiful?" she asks again.

My throat feels dry, constricted, but I manage to nod, manage to tell her, "Yes."

She comes closer. "So what's stopping us?"

This is it. This is the moment I can tell her or not tell her. Either way, everything changes. Either way, everything falls apart.

I open my mouth, but before I can answer, I see distant motion out of the corner of my eye. A helicopter, a war bird painted in the red and white of the warriors who serve the Theocracy. "Chopper," I say instead. "We can't be up here." It's still far enough away we haven't been spotted, but it's heading in our direction.

"Inside," Hannah says, taking my hand.

We duck into the building. Standing close—too close—in the hallway as the sound of the helicopter gets louder. It's right on top of us, flying low over the building, then it's gone and the only sound is the beating of our hearts.

"We're safe," I say.

"No," Hannah says, "we're not." I don't know what she means until she kisses me. Then I know. I know all too well.

"Hannah, we can't be here."

"I know," she says. "This is an apartment building. So it's got to have apartments. One of them must be vacant. One with a nice bedroom..."

"That's not what I mean."

"It's that girl, isn't it? That what's her name... Mark's sister, Lucy?" When I swallow hard and don't respond, she continues, "Is that it? You want to be with her instead? You can tell me, Andrus. I won't like it, but I'll understand."

"No, I mean... I like Lucy, and it's complicated, but I like you too."

"You can't have us both."

"I know. I don't want that."

"So what do you want?"

"I want... I want you, Hannah. I do. I love you, as much as I know what love is. I've never been good at it, never thought I'd find a girl for me, someone who could understand what it's like to be different..."

She kisses me. *Hard.* I kiss her back, not sure now what to do except maybe give in to this thing between us.

Hannah senses my confusion and pulls away. "There's something else. Something you're not telling me."

"Yes."

"If it's not Lucy, then what is it? You're not still worried about my dad, are you? He can't tell us what to do—at least not about this."

"It's about Hades and it isn't," I tell her. "It's about me."

"What about you, Rock Boy?"

I wish I could laugh and tease her back, but I can't. "Hannah, I shouldn't say. Your dad told me not to tell you."

Her eyes burn with curiosity. "Really? He said that? Now you have to tell me."

"There's a prophecy."

"So? There's a million prophecies." Her face drifts close, nuzzling my cheek.

"It's about me. Specifically."

"What does it say? That we shouldn't be together?"

"No, not that."

Her eyes search mine. "Then what? What is it? What could be so bad that my father doesn't want you to tell me? It's got to be pretty terrible if it's enough to keep you from wanting to be with me."

"It is... I'm going to die."

"What?"

"The prophecy says I'm supposed to sacrifice myself to defeat Cronus. I wasn't supposed to tell you because Hades was afraid if you knew, you'd try to change it. Because of the way we feel about each other."

She backs away, frowning.

"I'm sorry. I want to be with you, but I don't want to hurt you. Not if I'm going to die. And maybe Hades is right that you knowing will mess up his plans. Maybe I shouldn't have told you, but I couldn't—we couldn't—well, it would have been wrong not to tell you."

"But you did."

"Yeah."

She comes to me, no kiss this time, just an embrace that says everything I need to know. "Is that why you and Mark took so long at the elevator? Were you telling him too?"

"He thinks there might be another way to interpret the prophecy. He's going to get some books, see if he can find a way to fulfill the prophecy so I don't have to die."

"If there's a way," Hannah says, "then Mark's right. We have to find it."

I shrug. "What if there isn't?"

"Then I guess this is all the time we have. We should make good use of it..."

Her mouth covers mine, hungrier than ever, and I want to give in, want to just call it good with the truth I've given her. It's a truth I can live with, but I may not have to do that much longer.

"Hannah," I gasp between kisses, "how much do you know about your father's plans?"

"Enough."

"I don't mean about today, or the war. I mean what happens when he wins. To the people, to humanity."

She gives me a reassuring hug. "They'll be fine. Free to be what they want, like in Tartarus. Why?"

"Free because they'll be dead? Is that how Hades plans to rule? By killing everyone so they'll have to obey him?"

She steps out of the embrace, suspicion deepening the darkness in her eyes, eyes that flash a midnight black. "Who told you that?"

"Is it true?"

"He never mentioned it to me."

"Did you ask?"

"Well, no... I just assumed life would go on as it has, only different. Better."

"I had another dream. In Murder Town. Cronus was in it."

"He made you the offer again." There is no accusation in her words, just fact.

"Yes, but..."

"But what?"

"He told me Hades plans to kill everyone. Make them ghosts so they can never worship anyone else ever again. Including Ares. I don't know if I can trust your father. And I didn't... I wasn't sure I could trust you."

"Because I'm Hades' daughter?"

I nod.

"But you trust me now?"

I shrug. "I want to. I guess that depends."

"On what?"

"On what happens next."

"OK," she says. "Wait here." She swirls her cloak and turns to mist.

I watch Hannah drift away, not knowing where she's going, what she'll do, or if she'll come back. She never said she loves me. Never said why she was leaving. Just left me here, feeling vulnerable. Like a fool.

Was I right to trust her? A million paranoid "what ifs" careen through my head. *What if I never see her again?* What if I blew it, and not just to be with her, but what if I blew it for everyone? For Mark, for Lucy, my parents, and all the rest... What if Hannah is telling her father right now? Or going after Mark? Or a bunch of other stupid, crazy things...

I hate not knowing. I hate feeling helpless. And for the first time in a long time, I hate being alone.

I think back to what James, my white-haired old butler told me when I confessed I was falling in love with Lucy. He'd said, 'Love is a wonderful thing, but it's also selfish. It can destroy happiness as easily as it creates it.'

Confused, I'd asked, 'So you're saying I *shouldn't* love this girl?'

And James had replied, 'No, I'm saying *if* you love her, be sure the consequences won't leave her worse off than before she knew you.'

Is that what I've done? With Lucy? With Hannah? Has my love complicated things, ruined them beyond repair? I ask myself and have no answers.

31

THE LONGEST MOMENT OF MY LIFE

What happens when I die?

I never asked Ares or Hades. Titans and Gods aren't human. Our souls don't go to Tartarus, if we even have souls at all. But we go on in some manner, somewhere, as energy, at least for a while... but we only come back when people believe in us.

Worship us.

Who do I have like that? Ares has Mark. Hades has Hannah and all his ghosts. Cronus and the rest of the Titans have the entire NGT. Me, I might be a hero, but I'm nobody. I'm not famous. There are no myths about me, no legends. There is only truth, and the truth is, I will be forgotten.

The sound of the patrol copter comes back, buzzing overhead, then is gone again.

I begin to pace, begin to worry. A plan forms in my head: to go to the temple alone, to do what must be done without risking Mark, without risking Hannah. I know it's reckless, I know it's dumb, but it begins to sound better and better the longer Hannah is gone. It also sounds easier than waiting for her to tell me whatever she's going to tell me.

About her father. About her. About us.

I walk to the elevator, finger poised over the button. If I press it, my worries are over. Instead, I make a fist and punch the wall. That helps. Me, not the wall. There's a hole in it now to match the one in my heart.

"I wasn't gone *that* long," Hannah says from behind me. "Good thing you're a Titan because you make a lousy interior decorator."

She's back! And she's joking, so that's a good sign. Isn't it?

I brush drywall from my hand and arm, smiling sheepishly. "I was just messing around. Testing my strength. You know, in case I need to knock down some temple walls."

"Uh-huh." Hannah watches me, sharing my smile but not quite sharing it. Something is off.

"So what's up?" I ask.

She shrugs. "Had to check on a few things."

"Oh... Is, uh, everything all right?"

"Maybe. As much as anything can be in this messed-up world."

"I meant between us."

Now it's her turn to say, "Oh." She follows it with another shrug.

Neither of us says anything for what seems like minutes, but is only seconds. *The longest moment of my life.* Everything slows down in times like these. It doesn't matter whether you know it's going to be good or bad in the end. It's the moments before, the moments between knowing and not knowing, the moments of hope or fear that feel like forever.

This is one of them.

"We need to talk," Hannah says the three most dreaded words any female can utter.

"OK." I don't make any attempt to approach her. I just wait, glad the elevator is close in case I need to leave. It's funny how I can fight hordes of monsters yet the thought of facing Hannah fills me with a terror not even my worst enemies can bring.

"I love my father," Hannah pauses, waiting for my reaction. I'm not sure what my expression says, because I don't reply, just wait for her to continue. She sighs. "Hades is complicated. He's been through so much, Andrus. Much more than either of us, and we've been through a lot."

"Hannah..."

"No, let me finish." Another sigh. "I don't like that you would question my father's motives or his plan. I've spent my whole life believing in him, following his plan, doing what needs to be done. I've never doubted him. Not for an instant!"

"And now?"

"I looked into it. What you wanted to know."

"And?"

"I couldn't find any evidence to substantiate Cronus' claims."

"But did you ask him? Did you ask your father?"

"What? No! I can't do that. You know I can't."

"Then how do you know?"

"I don't, I just feel like he wouldn't, that's all. Look, I made subtle inquiries. I poked around. There was nothing, no hint of what you're talking about. I'm not going to give Cronus what he wants, Andrus. I'm not going to let his lies poison me against my own father. And you... you shouldn't let your father poison you against mine, or against me."

"I'm not against you." I take a step toward her, arms outstretched, but Hannah waves me off.

"No," she says. "I can't do that. Not now."

"I knew I shouldn't have said anything."

"You had what you believed to be a valid concern. I get that. And you trusted me enough to bring it up. I don't fault you for that. I'm not happy about it, but I understand. If I were you, I probably would have done the same."

I look from Hannah to the hole in the wall, then back to her again. "So what happens next?"

She raises an eyebrow. "Between us?"

"No. Well, I mean, yeah, I want to know, but it'd be stupid to ask that now. I mean what happens next with our plan. Are we ready to move on the temple?"

"In a minute," she says. "There's something I need to tell you first."

I brace myself, every part of me tensing for the worst. I'm facing a new army, only it's one of words, not monsters, and I know which kind I prefer.

Hannah says, "This is hard... You know how I said before I don't feel like my father would do the things you accuse him of?"

"I remember."

"Well, feeling and *knowing* are two different things."

A flicker of hope rises in me. "What are you saying?"

"I'm saying I'll keep my eyes open, just in case."

"And if it's true?"

"Then I'll do something about it. What, I don't know, and I hope I never have to find out. But I have a vested interest in making sure humanity doesn't die."

"You do?"

"Think hard, moron. I'm a demigoddess. You know, *half-human*."

"Oh! Right. Good point." I flash an awkward smile.

Hannah comes toward me, and I think—*I hope*—we'll embrace and all will be forgiven, but she walks right by and hits the down button on the elevator.

I was wrong about before. Waiting for the elevator is the longest moment of my life.

32

THE THINGS WE DO

WE'RE STANDING TOGETHER, yet so far apart. I sense the tension, the frustrated desire. It's in both of us. Hannah and I are going down—literally, in the elevator, but is our relationship going down too? I have to know.

"Hannah?"

"Yeah?"

I meet her gaze then look away. "Nothing, I... never mind."

The elevator keeps going down, sinking faster than my attempt to start a conversation. I can feel her eyes on me, feel the unspoken question between us.

"Andrus," she says, "whatever you want to tell me, this might be your last chance."

"I know." But now it's weird, like the moment has passed, and I'm not sure I have the words—*the right words*—to express myself. Not without making things worse. So I keep silent, watching the floor numbers light up as we pass them. I almost get up the nerve to talk to her—really talk—but now we're too close to the lobby.

"I'm sorry," is all I have time for.

"I know," she says.

The elevator opens, depositing us into the lobby. Tenants come, tenants go. One stands by the mail box, fretting over his monthly bills while a slave waters the potted plants. It's all so normal. Meanwhile, in another dimension, ghosts are bowling with severed heads. And that's normal too.

But what's normal for me? I don't feel like I belong in this world or Tartarus. Maybe I belong somewhere else, on some world in-between. It's not impossible. After the Gods War is over, I'd like to find out.

～

THE FIRST THING we do is get uniforms. Shadow has spotted a likely pair of targets not far from here. Hannah lures the warriors into an alley, one male, one female. She claims her friend's been injured by a mugger.

I play the role of the friend, lying on my side, keeping my face turned away until one of the warriors kneels to assist me. As soon as I feel his hand on my shoulder, I roll over and hit him so hard his helmet flies off. He bounces off the wall and goes down hard.

Meanwhile, Hannah pulls a chloroform-soaked cloth from her belt pouch. She gets the female in an armlock and forces the cloth over her face. Now there are two unconscious warriors. After we remove their weapons and uniforms, Hannah wants to slit their throats, but I won't let her.

"Not getting soft on me, are you?" she teases.

I haul the bodies to a rusty metal dumpster, heave them in, and shut the lid.

"This is dumb," she complains. "They'll just wake up and sound the alarm."

"Can't you do something? Some magic? What about one of those wards?"

Hannah mutters something under her breath, then fishes a stick of chalk out of her belt pouch. She hastily scrawls a protective ward on top on the dumpster, sealing them in with her magic. She gives me side eye the whole time.

"Satisfied?" she asks.

I nod. "Yeah, thanks. They're people, not monsters."

"People on the wrong side."

"I was too until a few days ago. Until you told me my destiny. Now look at me."

She shakes her head. "Saint Andrus the Merciful! Face it, Rock Boy: You can't save everyone."

She's right. It feels weird not killing the warriors when I've already dealt so much death, but this isn't like fighting monsters. Those two warriors are human. They've been lied to by the Theocracy, just like me. Maybe now they'll have a chance to learn the truth. Maybe not. Either way, they won't be able to interfere with our plan.

We strip down, changing into the stolen white togas and red cloaks that will allow us to walk into the temple. I don't know how I feel about wearing the uniform. This is what I wanted to be for so many years, and now it's something I can never be except as a disguise.

As we walk toward the end of the alley, I look back toward the dumpster. "Hey, Hannah?"

She sighs. "What now? You want to go back to tuck them in? Read them a bedtime story? The kind where everyone gets a happily ever after?"

"No. That's not what I... I mean, those two back there... they're not going to run out of air, are they?"

Hannah rolls her eyes. "Seriously? They're good; they're fine. It's a limited time ward that'll wear off in a few hours. But you shouldn't be concerned about them. Death is back. It's the new reality."

"What's that supposed to mean?"

"*People are going to die.* We're going to kill them—as many as it takes. But death is a gift. The ones we kill, they won't linger on. They won't be locked into false life and endless pain. They won't be zombies. They'll be at peace. And so will we, because they won't be around to stand in our way. You got me?"

"Yeah, I got you."

"Good..." Hannah looks like she's about to say something more.

There's something in her eyes, something almost on her lips, and I wonder if maybe we'll get to talk about our relationship after all. But then her warrior's radio crackles to life.

A female dispatcher comes over the line. "Unit 12, come in. Over."

Shit. I reach for the radio attached to the shoulder of my uniform, but my mind goes blank—which is all the more disturbing because I trained for this. I learned all the warrior response codes back at Axios... At least, I think I did. Maybe I daydreamed my way through that class as well.

Fortunately, Hannah grabs hers. "Unit 12," she replies in a curt, official tone that sounds like her yet not like her. "Over."

Static, then the dispatcher asks, "What's your 101? Over."

Now I remember... "101" means "What's your status?" It also means "Are you secure?"

"10-106," Hannah responds. *Status secure.* "Injuries minor; victims declined to file complaint. No sign of perp. Requesting code 7. Over."

"10-4, Unit 12," the dispatcher says. "Code 7 cleared. Enjoy your lunch. Dispatch out."

"I'm impressed," I remark in surprise. "You know your codes."

Hannah smiles. "Not my first time pulling this stunt. Probably won't be my last." Her voice is back to normal.

"What did you do? To your voice, I mean. You didn't sound like yourself."

"Hello? Magic. I'm a witch, remember? I can do anything... well, almost." She looks away when she says it, a sudden sadness crossing her face, then it's gone.

"I can't believe I froze up when dispatch came over the line. With all my warrior training too! I couldn't remember the response codes. Good thing you were here. I would have blown it for sure."

"You're not the same person you thought you were," she says. "The old Andrus is fading. It's only natural you'd forget. Besides, it's not like you haven't been through a lot."

"Is that... is that what happened to you? After you lost your mom and your dad was imprisoned? You couldn't be who you thought you were anymore? You had to become... something else?"

"I'll always be the daughter of Hades. What happened doesn't change that, just like what's happening to you doesn't stop you from being a Titan." Hannah pauses, and when she speaks again, her voice tight with emotion. "The things we do, they don't change *what* we are, they change *who* we are. The old Hannah wouldn't have had to train to avenge her father with the meanest ghosts in Murder Town. She would have been a spoiled princess in a castle. She wouldn't have been hunted, wouldn't have had to live like an animal one step ahead of the Titans. But the old me is dead. She's a ghost, Andrus. A ghost in my mind."

I nod. "I guess I'm going through the same thing. It's hard to see while it's happening. Everything's so confusing! It's like a pain—a real, physical pain. I'm losing myself, who I was, or thought I was. And I don't know what to do. I don't know whether I should slow the change down or speed it up."

She puts a hand on my shoulder. "You'll figure it out. Everyone does."

"Hannah..."

"Yeah?"

"There's one thing I've figured out."

"What's that?"

I take her in my arms and kiss her because I don't have words for what comes next. I only have this, and it might be the one thing that saves us. And if it doesn't, if it's our last kiss, then I want it to mean something. I want it to burn, to linger, to be something we'll always remember. And Hannah wants it too. She kisses me back. She kisses me and for a moment, time stands still.

When it's over, Hannah has to catch her breath. She's looking at me in a new way now, a better way. The sadness is gone.

I slip on my red-plumed helmet to complete my disguise. "Well?" I ask, posing for her. "How do I look? Dashing? Noble? Studly?"

She snorts. "You look like those brainwashed fascists in the dumpster."

"Perfect! Come on, Witch Girl. Let's be heroes."

33

DON'T BE A HERO

Walking up the steps to the Temple of the Unblinking Eye feels different. This time, I'm not coming to worship. I'm coming to save the people I love and maybe, just maybe, put a stop to the Theocracy's evil.

The first phase of our plan is simple: Get in, don't attract attention. But I grow more anxious with every step, fearing we'll be found out, that someone will recognize me and raise the alarm. I keep my eyes straight ahead, hoping the cheek plates of my helmet are enough to hide me from my enemies.

We've fallen in behind a group of warriors returning from patrol. All we have to do is blend in, then split off once we're inside.

I look at the sky. For one dizzying moment, the cloudless blue becomes gloom-brown: the cavernous ceiling of Tartarus with its million gems shining like stars. I feel like I'm back in the Underworld, or standing on the threshold. Like I could be anywhere in the universe, the dimensions flowing like the Styx, like some great unbroken cosmic river. Then Tartarus is gone.

The sun glares down. In the distance, birds cry. Traffic beeps. I'm still in Othrys. Still on Earth. I blink and stumble on the temple steps.

Hannah catches my arm before I can fall, and more importantly, before anyone notices. "You all right?" she whispers.

I nod. Maybe it was a hallucination. Maybe it was my new power manifesting. We're crossing over now, from the sunlit steps into the shadow of the temple. Could my power have been triggered by the wards? Some kind of weird magical fluctuation when our energies met?

Hannah would know the answer, but I can't ask her. This isn't the time or place to talk about it, and we likely won't get one once we're inside. That's when the second phase of our plan kicks in: We split up. Hannah will find and disable the wards, while I head to the dungeon. Once the wards are down, Hannah assures me they'll glow then fade to signal her success. That's my cue to get Mom, Dad, and Lucy out of the building and into the SUVs Hades will have waiting for us.

Hannah and I enter the temple—not the way citizens go to worship, but off to the left where the warriors have their barracks and administration. To the right is the Great Library and where the priests live. How I wish I could go over there now and kill Inquisitor Anton, his mad master, Archieréas Vola, and the other zealots. But that's not why we're here. Not today. That fight will come, just like the fight against Cronus.

Cool marble surrounds us as we proceed into the warrior wing. Hannah and I part ways, exchanging one last lingering look before giving ourselves over to the mission.

I follow the signs toward the dungeon. Warriors pass me by, red cloaks flapping in the frosty, air conditioned halls. We're doing it. This is really happening. And yet, there's a chill growing inside, a slow, sinister feeling that shivers up my spine.

It's not the air conditioning. *It's fear.* A fear that's different from battle. Fear that for all my power, I won't be able to save my loved ones. That I'm fooling myself and all I'm good at is destruction.

Didn't I destroy my parents' lives and Lucy's? I killed Mark. And if Cronus is right and Hades really does want to kill everyone, then by freeing him, I've destroyed this world. Maybe Gyges and I aren't so different. Maybe Titans like us are born to destroy. It's in our blood. Blood we shared and blood we spilled.

In a crazy way, I miss Gyges. I feel closer to him than I should. I wonder if I hadn't been sent to Earth, hadn't been disguised as a human, what I would have grown into had I remained in Tartarus... Would I have become something monstrous like Gyges? A battle-hungry creature unrecognizable to the people I know and love? A cannibal king like my father? Or would I still be some version of me?

These are questions I can't answer.

They are also things I can't think about, not if I want the mission to succeed. With dawning horror, I realize some small part of myself doesn't want to face my foster parents again, doesn't want them or Lucy to see what I've become. I worry I'll lose them. I'm worried I'll lose their love. But that's not a sure thing. If I stop now, if I don't follow through, then I really will lose them. Forever. And I can't have that.

I follow the signs deeper into the complex, the hallways leading past offices, past barracks and armories and training rooms, finally to stairs marked DUNGEON: AUTHORIZED PERSONNEL ONLY. I could take the elevator but I need to give Hannah time to disable the wards. I also want to familiarize myself with the layout. An elevator can be shut off or redirected to the wrong floor. A staircase can't. That could mean the difference between life and death.

No one has stopped me or spoken a word. I've exchanged a few nods with passing warriors, but that's it. That could change at any moment as I get closer to the dungeon. Assuming I get there. And once I do, once I see my parents and Lucy again, what do I say? I know what to do: *free them*. That part's obvious. It's covered in the plan. What's not covered is how they'll react—how any of us will react—and how that could impact our escape.

This is a lot to think about, so I run the different outcomes in my head: some happy, some bittersweet, but not once do I imagine a version where we aren't reunited. My brain simply can't wrap itself around that idea. I can imagine a dozen scenarios where the mission fails, where I'm unable to protect my parents and Lucy as we flee the building. But the thought that I might already be too late is so foreign, so destructive, it never enters my consciousness.

The dungeon is a lonely, wailing place of dark stone without any of the bright airiness or artistic touches of the upper levels. There's no point. It is a place of punishment for sins against the state, sins against the Titans. A place the doomed are sent to suffer until the final torture comes: *to be fed to Cronus*.

But I'm here. I can stop that. I can stop everything.

I stab and slash my way past the outer guards, killing them because I have no choice. I smash down the door. An alarm goes off, wailing loud—too loud—but it can't be helped. I kill several more guards before taking the head jailor hostage. It's all too easy.

I tell the jailor which prisoners I want. Demand to know what cells they're in. "Take me to them. Take me now or die!" Only he says he can't. The alarm shrills, louder than any harpy. I press my claws to his neck. "Don't be a hero," I warn.

"I—I'm not," he gasps. "The prisoners you want, they're... they're not here!"

"Where are they?" I work my claws deeper, drawing blood. It's all about control. A fraction of an inch more, and the man is dead. He knows it. I know it.

"S-someone..." the jailor stammers, "someone signed them out... transferred them to the temple."

"When?" I demand.

"Half... half-an-hour ago."

"Who?"

The man is shaking now. "Some inquisitor! I—I don't know his name."

But I do. Before I make the jailor punch up the prisoner transfer request on his computer, I already know the name I'm going to see: *Inquisitor Anton*.

34

A LITTLE TRICK

THE NEWS HITS ME like a punch to the heart. *Gone!* My parents and Lucy taken by that bastard, Anton. But it's why he's taken them that disturbs me most: He's taken them to be sacrificed!

Hannah doesn't know. I have to warn her.

I look down at the jailor, wondering why he's so quiet. It's because he's dead. In my shock, my claws extended, skewering his throat. When I yank the crystals free, blood gushes everywhere, splashing across the computer screen. Splashing across the names of my loved ones.

I hurl the jailor's corpse across the room. I want to smash his desk, smash the computer, smash everything! But I stop myself. I remember Hannah and reach for my radio. "Unit 12," I say, my mind remembering the codes Mr. Cross drilled into me. "What's your 20? Over."

"This is Unit 12," Hannah replies. "Switch to channel 4. Over."

I switch, assuming it's to a secure channel where dispatch can't eavesdrop on us. "Where you at? Over."

"Library. Ran into some problems. The wards are arranged in a sequential pattern, and if I disable them in the wrong order... well, it won't be good. They're trapped. I need more time, but I'm guessing that alarm means I'm not going to get it. Did you rescue your people?"

"Anton beat me to it. They're going to be sacrificed!"

"Andrus, I'm sorry! Do you need me to come help?"

"No, keep at those wards. I just had an idea..." I wipe blood from the computer screen. "Hannah?"

"Yeah?"

"Those wards... you said they're to keep things from getting in."

"That's right."

"Would they block me from tunneling inside the building?"

"You mean up to the temple?"

"Yeah. That alarm means things are going to get messy for me real fast, and I don't have time to fight all those warriors. Can I use my magic to punch through the floor and shortcut that way?"

"Gimme one second..."

"Hannah!"

Static. More static.

"What are you doing? What's taking so long?"

"Disabling the internal subset. They're on a different chain from the external wards. Almost there..."

I hear the sound of booted feet, the shout of angry men heading to the dungeon. "Can you hurry? I don't have a lot of time."

"Yes!" Hannah exclaims. "Got it. You should be good to go."

"Ok, good. Oh, and Hannah?"

"What?"

"There's one more thing I can do... something to buy us both time."

"What's that?"

"A little trick I learned in Murder Town..." I examine the list of prisoner names displayed on the computer screen., each trapped behind an electronically locked cage door. I remember what I did at the asylum and run my finger down the locking controls.

Cages clang open. Prisoners rush out.

"You're free!" I shout. "But you have to fight!"

35

YOU CAN'T SAVE EVERYONE

I TUNNEL UP through the dungeon floor. Below, the first wave of newly-freed prisoners snatch up weapons from the dead as the warriors close in. I wish I could do more, but there's no time to waste. Hannah said, 'You can't save everyone,' and she's right. But I can try to give those that matter a chance, no matter how slim—the chance to save themselves.

I break through to the ground floor. My arrival stuns the warriors in the lobby.

The smart ones run.

The dead ones don't.

Then I'm racing toward the temple. To my right, I see the marble steps leading down to the street. Three black SUVs glide into parking spots with clockwork precision. These must be the getaway vehicles Hannah promised. That's good. That's one less thing to worry about.

I slaughter the guards standing watch outside the temple. All pretense of mercy gone. Now there is only kill or be killed. My rage is a cold, frozen thing. I need to keep it that way. Sharp, focused. Under control. If I don't, if I can't, if I resort to the elemental savagery within... Bad things will happen. I know that now. And so I fight to control my rage, bend it, shape it, forge it into a weapon I can use instead of a weapon that uses me.

They've sealed the temple, bolting the massive steel door from within. They think that can keep me out. I try, but it's no good forcing it. I can't dig through the walls. My fingers penetrate the stone enough to grip it, but can't punch through. That means the outer wards are still active. How much more time does Hannah need?

I curse, casting my gaze around wildly. There! Above the temple doors, set high over the entrance—*a weak spot*. An elliptical stained glass window depicting the Unblinking Eye of Cronus. That's how I'll do it. That's how I'll get in.

Before I can climb, I hear booted feet. I whirl to find a pair of warriors rushing up the steps, back from patrol. They've witnessed me kill the others. They know I don't belong.

I raise my right fist and rocket a red crystal into each of them. Dead center kill shots. I'm recalling my weapons even before the bodies tumble down the steps. I jam the crystals back into my flesh, crack my knuckles, and climb.

The wall resists my magic, but only enough to prevent me breaking through. With enough effort—or maybe pure rage—I can get my fingers and boots to push in just enough to pull myself up. Below, people watch me climb. Pointing. Shouting. But no one stops me because no one can.

I'm at the giant stained glass eye. Hanging there, gathering my strength. I figure the glass is warded, but glass is glass. It's not stone. Whatever wards there are can't be as permanent or as powerful.

Gazing into the Eye, I see my father's cruel and cunning face staring back at me and I want to lash out. I want to kick it in.

I want to destroy!

So that's exactly what I do. The Eye shatters, glass erupting in a jagged, multicolored rain. It feels good. It feels like my entire life has been leading up to this moment. To standing up to the state, to my father, to everyone and everything. But something else happens too —some kind of toxic energy spills over me. Energy I can't see, but it feels like burning oil: hot, wet, and oozing. I shake it off, wondering what it was, but the magic doesn't hurt me, only makes me angrier.

I dive through the broken window, landing cat-like in the balcony overlooking the gallery. This is where the Losers sit during sermons and sacrifices. This is where Mark and Lucy sat the last time we were here, where they watched the Ritual of the Worm while I had a front row seat.

I rush to the balcony railing, my gaze sweeping over the gallery to the golden pulpit—the *bema*—that raised dais where Archieréas Vola preaches his blind devotion to the Titans. The bema is pulled back now as it was the last Sunday I was here—pulled back to reveal the sacrificial pit, the "Mouth" of Cronus into which the doomed are devoured.

My parents are there, gagged and chained. And Lucy is there: beaten, bloodied, her back bare. She's been whipped raw, her pale skin covered in angry red lines. She hangs high from the ceiling on the sacrificial chain, the holy meat hook through her back. She's dangling over the pit, the smoking hole that leads to the belly of Cronus.

Lucy looks dead, but isn't. Not yet. She squirms and shudders on the hook. A warrior stands by to work the controls that will lower her to her doom. Two more warriors hold swords to my parents' throats.

Inquisitor Anton stands nearby, looking imperious in his midnight blue cloak and azure robe. He wields his golden mace—the ceremonial club with a metal head in the shape of the Eye of Cronus.

"Andrus!" Anton shouts. "Andrus Eaves! Son of Cronus, we bid you welcome." The inquisitor smiles in that frightful way of a man who enjoys torture, who lives for it. He's middle-aged with thinning black hair, a slight paunch. Entirely unexceptional, except for the eyes—eyes that are fish-gray pools of nothing, reflecting only Anton's mad belief, his perverse desire to inflict suffering.

I feel my control slip, my rage threatening to boil over. "Let them go!" I yell. "Let them go, you bastard, or I swear I'll—"

"You'll do what? Watch them die? By the time you get to me, they'll be dead."

"And so will you," I warn. "You and your guards."

"We give our lives gladly for the glory of Cronus!" Anton says. "Although I admit death is a new and interesting concept... something else we have you to blame for." Anton clutches absently at his chest, his free hand pressing over the knife wound Lucy gave him at Axios. He grimaces. "Today," he grunts, "today is a day to repay old debts, to fulfill old promises."

I wrestle back rage. That's not the way. I need calm. *Icy calm.* I need control. I imagine myself in Tartarus, drowning my rage in the frozen waters of Lake Cocytus. Sinking my rage like a rock, like a red-hot stone to the murky green bottom. Slowly, I regain control enough to plot, to plan, not just to kill.

I calculate the odds of surviving a jump from this height. Not good, not without breaking my legs. No, there has to be another way. I have three spikes, one for each warrior, but while the two guarding my parents are close enough, by the time I'm able to target the third, he'll have had plenty of time to drop Lucy into the pit...

I could shoot Anton instead. Every part of me wants to. The rage wants to, wants to come bubbling up from the depths in all its berserk fury. It wants revenge. I want revenge, and Anton's the most satisfying target, a man I've dreamed of killing practically from the moment we met. A man who deserves to die. Horribly, hatefully, painfully. And yet he's the least important target, since he's not holding a blade to anyone's throat. But maybe if he dies, his guards will surrender... but I know that's unlikely. His men undoubtedly have orders to kill the prisoners if anything happens. No matter who I shoot, by the time I recall my crystals and rush downstairs, someone I love will be dead. What I need is time. Time to think, time to plan.

"Where's Archieréas Vola?" I demand. Maybe, if I keep Anton talking, some new opportunity will open up...

"The Great One was going to preside over the sacrifice personally, but your arrival changed that. Vola has been evacuated. He left me to deal with you."

"You mean he left you here to die!"

Anton shrugs. "If that is my fate... but no one has to die today,

Andrus. Not if you agree to join Cronus. I believe he made you an offer? One you would be wise not to refuse."

I don't answer. I look from my parents' tortured faces to Lucy's and back to Anton.

"It's a simple yes or no," the inquisitor says. "It has nothing to do with this…" He gestures with his mace to the prisoners. "Or even what's between us. I am big enough to put aside this grudge, this… *misunderstanding*… if that is Cronus' will."

"And if I'm not?" I call back with contempt.

Anton steps forward, arms spread like a martyr. "Then kill me! *Kill me, Andrus*. I am not afraid to die in service to what I believe. Can you say the same?"

That burning oil sensation comes crawling back, creeping over my skin, threatening to break my control. Again, I think of ice. Again, it retreats.

"The way I see it," Anton continues, "you have no choice but to accept. Say yes, Andrus! Yes is the easiest thing—the easiest thing in the world. One simple yes sets your parents free, saves sweet Lucy from her blessed fate…"

What the inquisitor says is true, but what he doesn't mention is it also damns me to be my father's slave, misusing my power to open new worlds for him to plunder. I can't do that. But if I don't… If I say no, can I live with what happens next?

"You can, of course, continue to resist," Anton says, "to be the reckless, entitled fool you've always been. Maybe you think you don't need anyone now that you know you're a Titan. Maybe you won't care if we lower Lucy into the pit…" He gestures to the warrior working the chain's controls.

Before I can think to shoot, he drops Lucy, just a few feet. Now her knees are level with Anton's head.

The inquisitor chuckles. "Did you think I was going to drop her all the way? Just like that? No, that was merely to get your attention." Anton returns his mace to the loop on his belt, then—wearily—steps behind the pulpit. He bends down and with that grimace on his face,

I can almost hear him hissing in pain. When he rises, I see what he has in mind.

The Worm-Maker. The gold-plated hacksaw he uses to cut off the legs of sinners, to make them "worms"—crawling, begging things. He reaches out and grabs Lucy by the ankle, bringing her leg toward him. Placing the saw against her skin.

"Say yes," Anton warns, "or don't. Either way, I win and Cronus feasts—on her soul or the souls of millions. It's your choice. Be the Bridge Between Worlds or bear witness to the deaths of everyone you love!"

I look at Lucy. Blonde. Beautiful. Proud, even in chains.

I look at my foster parents, George and Carol Eaves. The people who raised me, the people who love me.

I see them all and know what I must do.

36

THE MISSING PART

As if by some miracle, the once-invisible wards glow. Walls, floor, ceiling. All around the temple, mystic symbols flare, then fade away.

She did it! Hannah did it.

The inquisitor and his men react in shock. This is it, the sign I'm making the right decision. I take advantage of the confusion, firing a crystal at the warrior working the chain's controls. He goes tumbling away in a heap.

I fire at Anton, but at the last second, the bastard dodges, turning what should have been a kill shot into a flesh wound. My spike takes him through the arm instead of the ribs. But it's the arm holding the Worm-Maker; the golden hacksaw falls from his nerveless fingers, clattering into the pit.

I can't get a good shot at the two guards threatening my parents, so I don't try. Instead, I grip the balcony's railing, feeling my earth magic build, the power rising. I redirect the energy from me into the foundations of the temple. The building shakes, cracks appear in the walls. I pour more energy in, the entire temple vibrating, then I run. I run down the balcony steps: feet thudding, heart hammering.

I burst into the gallery. What I find doesn't make sense. The warrior guarding my father has run the other one through. The remaining warrior stands there, stiffly, eyes rolled up in his head. I get it: Now that the outer wards are down, he must be possessed by one of Hades' ghosts. My parents are out of danger.

But Lucy isn't safe—she's still hanging from the chain. Unlike my parents, she doesn't need a ghost to save her, and I'm not even sure she needs me. There's new life in her, new fight. She's wrapped her legs around Anton's neck. Choking him. Dragging him relentlessly toward the pit. The inquisitor gurgles, clawing at her whip-scarred legs with his one good arm. He shouldn't have lowered her. He shouldn't have gotten close. Not after all the things he's done to her and her family.

I race forward. If I can get there in time, I can still make this work. I can still save Lucy. I call her name, tell her to let him go. But Lucy doesn't listen. She's too deep in her hate now. Too lost in revenge. It's killing her.

I fire the last of my spikes. The shot rips through Anton's guts. The inquisitor releases his grip, and Lucy succeeds in dragging him over the edge of the pit. Only then does she release him.

It's a long way down. Anton screams, a high-pitched wail that echoes through the crumbling temple like the death-cries of the people he's sacrificed. Now he gets to serve his master one last time —as food.

"I did it," Lucy gasps. "I killed him!"

"You did," I say. I've never been prouder of her than I am in this moment. Maybe now she can know peace. Maybe now she can live the life Anton denied her. There's a spark in her, this beautiful, impossible girl who came from nothing, and I love her for it. "Hang on," I tell her. "Let's get you down from there."

She nods, grateful tears streaming from her eyes. "I knew you'd come... I knew."

Furtive movement catches my eye. The guard who'd been working the chain, the one I thought I'd killed, isn't dead. He's dragged himself back to the controls. I'm out of spikes, out of hope. Lucy and I share one last, anguished look before the warrior sends her plummeting into the pit.

I tear the golden pulpit free from the floor and send it hurtling into the wounded man, smashing him to pulp. I rush to the controls, hauling back the lever, halting Lucy's descent. Smoke and cinders fly out of the pit, but I hear Lucy cry my name, so I know she's not dead. There's still time. Time to undo this nightmare. Time to make things right.

"You!" I shout to the possessed guard. "Get my parents out of here!"

The man's eyes regain their focus and he signals me he's heard with a stiff nod. He moves to free my parents from their chains with the keys on his belt.

"Lucy!" I yell. "Hold on! I'm going to pull you up." I begin working the controls, hauling up on the chain hooked into her back.

Part of the ceiling caves in, smashing the pews my family sat on just days ago.

"Son!" my dad says, suddenly at my side. "We have to go! We have to get out of here. The whole place is coming down!"

"You and mom go. There are SUVs outside; they'll get you safe. I'm going to stay. I'm going to save Lucy."

"Andrus?" Mom says. "Andrus, honey! Please..."

"Take them!" I shout to the possessed guard. "Now!"

He hustles them toward the exit. My parents protest, but they go. I keep hauling the chain. Only when I hear the crash of falling stone do I look up. Just in time to see the ceiling rain down over the doorway. Down, onto my parents. Mom, Dad, the guard—all gone. Buried under dust and stone. And it's my fault. Mine!

I killed my parents.

I thought I could control my power, thought I could use it for good. The truth is, there is no controlling it. No controlling me. I'm a Titan, like Gyges. Like my father. I only know how to destroy.

Sorrow eats into my icy calm, then rage. A white-hot rage that comes rising, ripping into my defenses. A blind rage that tells me I can't save anyone, not even myself.

The chain slips through my fingers. *The chain.* Lucy! She's still alive. I can still save her, can still do one good thing if I can just hang on. I renew my grip, but something's wrong. Where there should be slack, now there's resistance. Like when you're fishing and latch on to a fighter. *A big one.* The chain rattles. The controls shriek in protest, then break. I lose my grip. The chain goes down. Lucy goes down.

Down into that smoking, flaming hell.

Down, into Tartarus.

Into Cronus.

I grab hold of the chain before it's gone, wrap the end of it around my wrist and pull. I dig my heels in, using all my magic to root myself to the spot. The chain rips my hands raw as the force in the pit greedily tugs at it. Just when I think I'm about to lose my grip, the resistance ends. I pull the chain up, but the weight doesn't feel the same. It doesn't feel right.

A minute later, I find out why. Only half of Lucy is left. Her legs are gone, chewed off like a shark's been at her—or my father, Cronus, with his shark-toothed grin. I hold Lucy in my arms, shake her until her sky-blue eyes open and she knows I tried.

I don't think, don't hesitate. I kiss her. I let that be the last thing she sees, the last thing she feels in this cold, cruel world.

Dark and powerful laughter comes booming out of the pit, malevolent in its mirth.

My rage returns—wilder, more reckless than before, and my vision swims with tears. It isn't fair! This isn't how it's supposed to be. We were all going to walk out into the sun together, Lucy, my parents, and me.

"Andrus?" my radio crackles with Hannah's voice. "Andrus, what's happening? Did you rescue your parents?"

I wipe the tears from my eyes. "They're dead," I reply. "Lucy's dead. Tell Mark I tried."

"I'm sorry! I'm so sorry, Andrus, but we have to go. The sun's going down. The monsters will be out soon..."

"The sun's already down."

"What? Andrus? You're not making sense!"

"For me," I say. "The sun's down for me. I don't want to live anymore."

"Andrus, no! Please, we need you. I need you!"

"I'm going to kill Cronus," I tell her. "I'm going to destroy everything, then myself. It's the only way. I'm sorry we can't be together, but I only get the people I love killed. I won't let that happen to you."

Static. Her voice comes back, tinged with pain. "Andrus, don't do this."

I ignore her. I walk over to the dead guard, the one I bludgeoned with the pulpit. I pull the crystal spike out of him and push it back into me. I flex my fingers. Make a fist. A killing fist.

"Either you come out," Hannah says, "or I'm coming in. Whatever you're planning, we can face it together—"

"Hannah?"

"Yes?"

"Don't. Don't come in. I don't want you to see this."

"Andrus, listen to me! You're not thinking straight. I know a lot's happened, but you need to get out of there, OK? If you won't do it for yourself, then do it for me."

"This is for you." I tear the radio off and throw it into the pit.

There's a moment's regret, a moment's doubt, then no choice. I surrender to rage: ancient, primal, molten. The lava of hate, the lava of pain. A weapon forged when the first spark of life came into me, into the earth, into the land. A weapon from beyond space, beyond time.

Me. I am that weapon.

I will pull apart this temple and reach down into that pit to kill my father, to destroy Cronus once and for all. It doesn't matter he's in another dimension. It doesn't matter where he is. I will get to him. I will find him and have my revenge...

I reach down into the pit with my mind, my magic, my hate. I reach down, determined to tear my father from his home, to bring him to me, where I can pit my rage against his. But Cronus is stubborn. He will not come. He only laughs. Whatever wards Hannah removed from the temple, she did not remove from the pit. And since I cannot uproot Cronus from his lair, I will send my rage to him. Send it all. Wave upon wave of hate, wave upon wave of suffering.

Down, into the pit. Blasting through wards. Blasting through everything.

I'm going to bring it down. I'm going to bring it all down! The whole damned temple. I'm going to hurl it from Earth right into Cronus' face. We'll see who's laughing then!

New energy surrounds me. Shimmering red energy coming from the crystal in my hand. The strange, stolen crystal I had to have because it felt like part of me.

Because it is part of me.

The missing part—the part that opens the door from one dimension to the next, that makes me the Bridge Between Worlds. The crystals and rage combined. *This is power!* The power I want, the power I need to win the Gods War.

Life doesn't matter. Death doesn't matter. There is only now, only sacrifice! Crimson energy courses through me, a fire as red as my rage, a fire that burns just as fast and twice as hot. It is an energy that once summoned, must be used.

Chunks of ceiling shatter down. Jagged lines erupt from the floor, spewing flames. The new energy flows through me, opening the Bridge, the Door, the Gate. It's beautiful. It's terrible. It's me and it's mine. But like everything in my life, I only have a moment to appreciate the result. The temple falls, collapsing over me like a tomb.

A tomb for the living.

A tomb for the dead.

I accept and embrace it.

When Death comes, it comes as a gift.

∼

DID YOU ENJOY THIS BOOK?

If you did, please take a moment to **leave a review**. Even just a single short sentence will help this book reach new fans!

Our heroes return in *The Gods War, Book IV*
— TITAN: RESURRECTION —

SPECIAL FREE BOOK OFFER

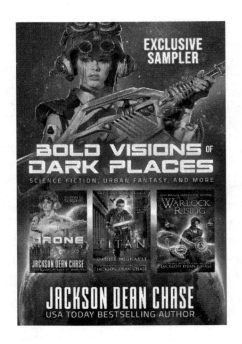

— FREE EXCLUSIVE SAMPLER —

BOLD VISIONS of DARK PLACES

featuring the best new sci-fi, urban fantasy, and more

by USA TODAY bestselling author

JACKSON DEAN CHASE

Get your free book now at

www.JacksonDeanChase.com

AFTERWORD
IF YOU ENJOYED THIS BOOK, PLEASE WRITE A REVIEW!

THERE'S NO DOUBT: War changes us. It takes who we are—or thought we were—and shatters us, rebuilding us into something new. If we're lucky, it changes us into something better. If we're not, well, that's where some of the greatest horrors of our world come from, whether they're Gods, Titans, or people.

Especially people.

We wanted to explore that in our series, and Book III really brings that home. We see the trauma, the deep wounds in our characters. Psychic scars that may never heal. We see what happens to those driven by revenge. Even when they win, they lose. If not the battle, then some vital piece of themselves. Maybe their life. Maybe even their soul.

Whoa! OK, that was heavy... but themes usually are. Let's move on to the fun stuff, talking about the characters and locations. Which are your favorites? **Write a review** so everyone knows!

We've had some great fan mail saying either Mark or Hannah is their favorite. That may be one of the reasons we split the characters up so much—to give Mark and Hannah room to breathe and to deepen their friendships with Andrus. Also, having only one or the other present means Andrus will get very different advice and assistance both in and out of combat.

Since Mark's possession by Ares forced him to stay submerged for most of Book II, we wanted to make up for that in Book III. Even when he gets repossessed, now it's Ares who stays submerged except in emergencies.

Probably the hardest decision was sending Hannah off on a sidequest with Hades and Cerberus. But it made sense she would want to spend time with her father, and from a story angle, it tied in with upping her skill level in dealing with high-level wards... something that becomes crucial when the heroes assault Cronus' temple.

One of the problems writing in first person is our villains rarely get much "screen time" except through direct confrontation with the hero. That makes it difficult to insert major adversaries like Nessus, Gyges, and Anton.

That's because their appearance automatically results in a fight or flight situation, and we only have room for so many of those per book. For minor adversaries like Blake and Brenda, it's also a question of balancing how much space to give them. While they add a certain flair to the story, they can't advance the plot the same way major enemies can.

Allied characters like Ares and Hades present special problems; these Gods are so super-powered that we have to either place limits on their ability to act or limit their screen time. As the Gods War heats up, however, we'll have no choice but to bring these Gods onstage more often, as well as the Titans...

Moving on to locations, how about that Greek underworld? Murder Town was a joy to write. The original plan was for our heroes to explore it in Book II, but as the word count grew, the best we could do was tease it, knowing the payoff would have to wait until Book III.

Andrus and Mark's time in Murder Town was originally supposed to last maybe three to six chapters, but once we got into it, we realized that wasn't nearly enough. A location like that simply has too much potential *not* to take up the space it does. It was also the only real chance we had to bring back Book I characters like Herophilos,

Blake, and Brenda... *poor Brenda!* She really got a raw deal in Book I. Hopefully, we left her ghost in a good place (not literally, since she's still in Murder Town, but spiritually). Maybe now, with Blake's hold over her gone, her soul can move on...

There are all kinds of fun places to explore in Tartarus and beyond—some of which you've seen, some of which you've only glimpsed. Others won't be revealed until later. Each book in the series requires new world-building. Even when we revisit existing locations like Othrys and the Temple of the Unblinking Eye, there's always something new to see—from the Museum of Failure to the underground dungeon.

Rest assured, our series will continue the tradition of exploring new worlds and new characters while revisiting fan favorites. It's a pleasure and privilege to bring you these stories. Thank you for taking the adventure with us!

— Daniel Mignault & Jackson Dean Chase

Did you enjoy this book?

If you did, please take a moment to **leave a review**. Even just a single short sentence will help this book reach new fans!

GLOSSARY

NEWLY REVISED AND UPDATED FOR THIS BOOK

- **Acheron:** The River of Woe, one of the five rivers of the Underworld. Acheron's waters are red with an oozing, blood-like consistency. The river serves to separate the good and peaceable ghost population from the malevolent half in places like Murder Town. Pronounced ACK-uh-ron.
- **Anton:** A ruthless member of the Inquisition and priest of Cronus. He was responsible for exposing Andrus as the son of Cronus, for raping Mark's sister, Lucy, and for the murders of Blake and Brenda. Lucy stabbed him at the end of Book I: *Titan*, but failed to kill him.
- **Archieréas:** The high priest of Cronus who serves as administrator, pope, and president of the New Greece Theocracy. The current office holder is Enoch Vola. Pronounced Ar-CUH-ray-us.
- **Ares:** God of War, son of Zeus. Pronounced AIR-eez.
- **Bridge of Burnt Souls:** A bridge connecting the Cliffs of Pain that overlooks the Phlegtheon. It was broken when Andrus battled Gyges in Book II: *Kingdom of the Dead*.
- **Cerberus:** The former guardian of the gates of Tartarus,

Hades' faithful three-headed monster dog. Pronounced Ser-BUR-us.
- **Cliffs of Pain:** Towering cliffs of volcanic black rock that lie beyond Murder Town. The cliffs are separated by the Phlegethon, but connected via the Bridge of Burnt Souls.
- **Cocytus:** The River of Wailing. Its icy waters end in a frozen lake in the depths of Tartarus where Hades imprisoned the defeated Titans. Hades' castle is built on a mountain of volcanic rock rising up from the lake's center. Cronus rules there now. Pronounced Ko-SIGH-tus.
- **Cronus:** King of the Titans, father of the Greek Gods. His symbol is the Unblinking Eye. Pronounced CROH-nus.
- **Day Patrol:** Armed bands of human warriors that serve as police; they answer to the priesthood.
- **Gaia:** The Earth Mother. She created the Titans with her lover, Ouranos, the Sky Father. Pronounced GUY-yuh.
- **Gyges:** One of the Lesser Titans and one of three brothers, all giants with fifty heads and a hundred hands who guard the gates of Tartarus in Cerberus' absence. Pronounced GUY-ghez.
- **Gods War:** The final battle between the Greek Gods and Titans in which the Gods lost and were either killed or imprisoned in Tartarus.
- **Hades:** Greek god of Death and the Underworld, older brother of Zeus. His symbol is the bident (a two-pronged trident). His imprisonment at the end of the Gods War prevents anyone from dying, but not from aging or becoming diseased or injured (see zombie). Pronounced HAY-dees.
- **Lethe:** The River of Forgetfulness. Its venomous green waters cause any one, ghost or mortal, who touches them to instantly and forever forget who they are and why they would ever want to leave Tartarus. Pronounced: LEETH.
- **Losers:** A popular insult, and also the name of the lowest free caste in society. Most slaves live better.

- **Loserville:** Slang for the run-down, economically challenged area of East Othrys; its population are insultingly referred to as "Losers."
- **Lucy Fentile:** Mark's sister, who sacrificed her scholarship and promising future in order to ensure her brother's. She is a love interest of Andrus. At the end of Book 1, she stabbed Inquisitor Anton and helped Andrus and Mark escape. Her current status is unknown.
- **Murder Town:** A city in Tartarus filled with the ghosts of murderers and their victims.
- **Nessus:** A centaur and captain of the Night Patrol who has a special hatred for Andrus. His brothers are Democ and Ruvo.
- **New Greece Theocracy (NGT):** An oppressive regime built on what's left of America after the Gods War destroyed much of the rest of the world. The NGT runs along what was the west coast, from Washington state to California. The Titans used their magic to transform its climate to match that of the Mediterranean.
- **Night Patrol:** Armed bands of human-hating monsters that enforce the after dark curfew. Mostly made up of centaurs and harpies.
- **Othrys:** Capital city of the NGT; named after Mount Othrys in Greece, birthplace of the Titans and their former capital on Earth. Previously known as Los Angeles. Pronounced AWTH-rees.
- **Ouranos:** The Sky Father. Lover of Gaia, the Earth Mother. Devoured by their son, Cronus. Pronounced OR-raw-nos.
- **Pankration:** A form of mixed martial arts practiced by the warriors of the NGT. It combines boxing and wrestling, with lots of takedowns, chokes, and joint locks.
- **Phlegethon:** The River of Flame. It's "waters" consist of flaming lava. It leads to Lake Cocytus. Pronounced FLEG-uh-thon.

- **Poseidon:** Lord of the Sea. Brother of Zeus and Hades. His symbol is the trident. Pronounced POH-sigh-dun.
- **Prometheus:** One of the few Titans who sided with the Gods during the Gods War. He was later punished by Zeus and imprisoned for daring to gift mortals with fire and wisdom. His current status is unknown. Pronounced PROH-mee-THEE-us.
- **Rich-O:** Loser slang for the wealthy caste.
- **Styx:** The River of Hate and Promises. Its monster-filled waters are black like oil and serve as a conduit between the world of the living and Tratarus, the Kingdom of the Dead. Pronounced: STICKS.
- **Tartarus:** The Kingdom of the Dead, home to ghosts and monsters. It was once ruled by Hades but now Cronus rules in his place. Pronounced TAR-tuh-rus.
- **Zeus:** King of the Gods, ruler of Mount Olympus, brother of Hades, and son of Cronus. His symbol is the lightning bolt. Pronounced ZUICE.
- **Zombie:** A person who should be dead but isn't, often with a traumatic brain injury. Zombies are doomed to wander in pain for eternity—or until Hades is freed from his prison.

MORE GREAT BOOKS TO ENJOY

THE BEST URBAN FANTASY AND SCIENCE FICTION

NEW NOVELS BY

DANIEL MIGNAULT & JACKSON DEAN CHASE

THE GODS WAR — *Urban Fantasy Series*

- Book 1: *Titan*
- Book 2: *Kingdom of the Dead*
- Book 3: *Gift of Death*
- Book 4: *Resurrection* (releases Fall 2018)

EXCITING NEW NOVELS BY USA TODAY BESTSELLING AUTHOR

JACKSON DEAN CHASE

BEYOND THE DOME — *Science Fiction Series*

- Book 1: *Drone* (releases Fall 2018)
- Book 2: *Warrior* (releases Fall 2018)
- Book 3: *Elite* (releases Fall 2018)
- Book 4: *Human* (releases Fall 2018)

JON WARLOCK, WIZARD DETECTIVE — *Urban Fantasy Series*

- Book 1: *Warlock Rising* (releases Fall 2018)
- Book 2: *Warlock Revenge* (releases Fall 2018)
- Book 3: *Warlock Reborn* (releases Fall 2018)

Want a free book? Go to www.JacksonDeanChase.com

ABOUT DANIEL MIGNAULT

Daniel Mignault started in the entertainment industry from a young age as an actor and model surrounded by worlds of fantasy and imagination.

As Daniel grew older, he found his passion change from being in front of the camera to creating the stories and characters he once played. Now a full-fledged writer, Daniel is ready to bring his stories to life.

Titan is his debut novel.

CHECK OUT DANIEL'S FILMS AND VIDEOS

Visit his IMDB page or YouTube channel.

For more information:
www.danielmig.com
www.imdb.com/name/nm3693355

amazon.com/author/danielmignault
facebook.com/danielmignaultauthor
twitter.com/DanielMignault
instagram.com/officialdanielmignault

ABOUT JACKSON DEAN CHASE

Jackson Dean Chase is a USA TODAY bestselling author and award-winning poet. His fiction has been praised as "irresistible" in *Buzzfeed* and "diligently crafted" in *The Huffington Post*. Jackson's books on writing fiction have helped thousands of authors.

From the author: "I've always loved science fiction, fantasy, and horror, but it wasn't until I combined them with pulp thrillers and *noir* that I found my voice as an author. I want to leave my readers breathless, want them to feel the same desperate longing, the same hope and fear my heroes experience as they struggle not just to survive, but to become something more." — JDC

Get a free book at www.JacksonDeanChase.com
jackson@jacksondeanchase.com

- amazon.com/author/jacksondeanchase
- bookbub.com/authors/jackson-dean-chase
- facebook.com/jacksondeanchaseauthor
- instagram.com/jacksondeanchase
- twitter.com/Jackson_D_Chase

A JON WARLOCK SUPERNATURAL THRILLER

WARLOCK REBORN

USA TODAY BESTSELLING AUTHOR
JACKSON DEAN CHASE

SACRIFICE TO
SURVIVE

DRONE
BEYOND THE DOME BOOK 1

JACKSON DEAN CHASE
USA TODAY BESTSELLING AUTHOR

FIGHT YOUR
FUTURE

ELITE
BEYOND THE DOME BOOK 3

JACKSON DEAN CHASE
USA TODAY BESTSELLING AUTHOR

EVERY WORLD ENDS

HUMAN

BEYOND THE DOME BOOK 4

JACKSON DEAN CHASE

USA TODAY BESTSELLING AUTHOR

SPECIAL FREE BOOK OFFER

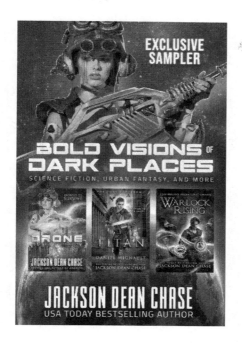

— FREE EXCLUSIVE SAMPLER —

BOLD VISIONS of DARK PLACES

featuring the best new sci-fi, urban fantasy, and more

by USA TODAY bestselling author

JACKSON DEAN CHASE

Get your free book now at

www.JacksonDeanChase.com

Made in the USA
Lexington, KY
19 November 2018